"Get down!"

Strong arms wrapped around her and a sturdy chest broke her fall as Briggs rolled with her onto the ground. In an instant, he had covered her frame with his own much larger one and drawn a gun she hadn't noticed until now from his waistband.

There was shouting, and Security rushed toward the section of the building Briggs had aimed at. Had shots been fired? She wasn't sure, but she thought so based on Briggs's reaction.

A figure clad in all black was running away, a high-powered rifle with a scope dangling from one arm. The chaos around her was overwhelming. She fought the urge to shrink into a ball.

Briggs helped Madison to her feet and grasped her hand, almost dragging her across the airport.

"Wait! My father!" She was gasping, everything happening too fast.

"We aren't leaving him. I have to get you out of range. The laser beam was on *your* head."

Sommer Smith teaches high school English and loves animals. She loves reading romances and writing about fairy tales. She started writing her first novel when she was thirteen and has wanted to write romances since. Her three children provide her inspiration to write with their many antics. With two dogs and a horse to keep her active in between, Sommer stays busy traveling to ball games and colleges in two states.

Books by Sommer Smith

Love Inspired Suspense

Under Suspicion
Attempted Abduction
Ranch Under Siege

Visit the Author Profile page at LoveInspired.com.

INDEX

RANCH UNDER SIEGE

SOMMER SMITH

LOVE INSPIRED SUSPENSE
INSPIRATIONAL ROMANCE

LOVE INSPIRED® SUSPENSE
INSPIRATIONAL ROMANCE

ISBN-13: 978-1-335-73623-9

Recycling programs
for this product may
not exist in your area.

Ranch Under Siege

Copyright © 2022 by Sommer Smith

For questions and comments about the quality of this book, please contact us
at CustomerService@Harlequin.com.

Love Inspired
22 Adelaide St. West, 41st Floor
Toronto, Ontario M5H 4E3, Canada
www.LoveInspired.com

Printed in U.S.A.

He that dwelleth in the secret place of the most High
shall abide under the shadow of the Almighty.
—*Psalm* 91:1

This book is dedicated to my mother with extreme gratitude.
Mom, you have always supported me no matter what
and provided a beautiful example in every way.
Words could never express how much you mean to me.
I love you BIG always!

ONE

Madison felt the eyes on her again.

She glanced around the crowded plane, but no one seemed to be looking in her direction. It was eerie.

She turned to gaze out the window, thankful she wasn't stuck out on the aisle, and studied the dirty snow piled along the sides of the tarmac. At least it wasn't snowing again now. She was glad to be headed south, even if only for the weekend. Early spring made her impatient for better weather, especially living up north where it was so much colder.

She turned to survey her fellow passengers once more, still aware of someone focused on her. No one stood out, though, so she was surely being ridiculous.

The flight attendant smiled at her as she passed, and the seats continued to fill. Madison didn't know whether to breathe a sigh of relief or become more concerned as the jet began to creep along the runway.

She hadn't felt safe since the attack in Boston.

It had seemed random at the time. She had been walking down the street, headed home to her apartment after staying late at the office. It was dark, and the street was quiet. Someone grabbed her from behind and tried to drag her into the alley. Thankfully, a passerby had noticed her struggle and ran up just in time, frightening the man away.

Madison had been shaken to her core. The police had insisted she was a random mugging victim, but she felt it was more than that, which made the lingering feelings of violation harder to shake. Ever since, she was anxious about being alone and often thought, like she did right now, that someone was watching her. She was off-balance, positive there was something more behind the attack. Every time she closed her eyes, she felt the grasp of her attacker again.

It was horrible.

The other worry plaguing her was her father. She hadn't seen him once in the three long years since her mother's death. They had disagreed over Madison's choices at the time, and while Madison could now see the error in her thinking, she hadn't at the time. For her, being successful had meant she had to leave and make a name for herself. She'd wanted to prove that someone raised on a ranch in Oklahoma could be just as successful as someone raised in the suburbs.

She had argued with her father and mother both, telling them she had to do more than they'd done with their lives, not knowing how she had hurt them with her words. She'd stayed long enough to finish college, get her start as a news reporter in the suburbs of Oklahoma City and see her mother begin to waste away from the horrors of cancer.

After the funeral was over, she'd hopped a plane to Boston to work her way into her dream job. She hadn't risked a return since then. If the truth were told, she had avoided going home. With her mother gone, and the death of a close friend a little over a year ago, she didn't look forward to the feeling of loss that would await her there. When Madison had learned of her friend Wade's death in Afghanistan, she hadn't even attended the funeral, making excuses that she couldn't fly out. She regretted that now.

But a visit was long overdue.

Her father had just been diagnosed with a heart condition, and doctors were still adjusting his treatment plan. Once she'd learned about his heart attack, she'd dropped everything to book a trip back to Oklahoma. She had no idea if her father was truly hoping to see her, but she would likely know how he felt for sure as soon as she arrived.

In the few times they had spoken since she'd left, the conversation had been stilted and rife with unease. She had tried to apologize over the phone, but such an impersonal apology was never the same. With his health issues, she dared not wait any longer. She had to make sure things were right.

For now, though, she needed to settle in and get some of her assignments done. She didn't want to have to write during her time at the ranch with her father.

Trying to work didn't distract her at all.

She felt someone watching her again, and looking all around the plane did nothing to help. Her skin crawled, and her insides roiled.

Going to her email inbox, she noticed an odd sender name with an attachment. Thinking it might be something she could use for the article she was writing, she opened it.

In the email attachments, however, videos of her own apartment appeared. Various views of her living quarters displayed her own form going about her daily life, making a sandwich, doing laundry, feeding her cat and her Pomeranian…

She slammed the laptop closed, startling a middle-aged woman next to her. She tried to smile at her in apology, but it fell short. Her hands trembled. She rose to go to the restroom, excusing herself robotically on her way to the aisle. Knees weak, everything around her faded into the surreal as she tried to hold it together walking down the aisle of the plane.

In the tiny airplane lavatory, she turned on the cool water and splashed some onto her face before staring at her reflection. She had to calm herself down. Airport security was tight, so surely no one could attack her on a plane. When she reached the Oklahoma City airport, her father would be there waiting for her.

She took deep breaths to clear her mind and slid down the door until she was sitting on the floor. Someone tried the door, prompting her to action. She scrambled up from the floor, feeling melodramatic at being caught in such a position. Opening the door to a young girl waiting impatiently, she tried to smile at her before she made her way back down the aisle to her seat.

Her laptop lay inconspicuously where she had left it, so she picked it up, sat down and opened it. She sent a text to her supervisor, Davis Denny, and he answered right away, promising to report the incident to the authorities. He told her not to worry, that he would make sure it was handled and that the police would secure her apartment. She tried to believe him and get it off her mind. Her thoughts still reeled, though.

Madison was thankful when the announcement was made that the plane was approaching the Oklahoma City airport, and passengers should turn off all electronic devices. She had seen enough.

The attack had occupied her thoughts all the way through the flight. No matter how thoroughly she examined it, she could think of no reason someone would want to hurt her, but she couldn't shake the feeling someone did. Why was she being targeted?

It was a mystery.

As the plane touched down, Madison

took a deep breath and did her best to put the whole thing out of her mind. Whoever was tormenting her was in Boston, so at least she should be able to relax here in Oklahoma for the weekend. She could figure it all out when she returned. Right now, she wanted to make everything right with her father. Who knew how much time they had left? Heart disease was a tough thing to overcome. He was blessed to survive his first heart attack.

Madison stepped into the airport to find her father waiting. He'd aged a lot in the years since she had last seen him. A slight pallor announced his lingering illness, and her throat tightened up in response. She stepped into his arms, glad to find them open as soon as he saw her. She was only vaguely aware of the stranger who stood beside him, watching her.

"Oh, Dad, I'm sorry it's been so long." She whispered it, but by the way the stranger shifted his weight, she knew he'd heard. When he backed away farther to give them some space, it confirmed her suspicions. And she was grateful.

"I'm sorry too, sweet pea. I should have insisted you come home sooner, but I didn't wanna stand in the way of your success." His pat on the back was achingly familiar.

Her father's voice sounded more gruff and tired than she remembered it. She smiled up at him, emotion overtaking her. "It was folly on my part. I didn't want to face Mom's absence. I made so many mistakes and bad decisions. And then Wade was killed, and it was just too much. I used my career as an excuse not to come home, and I'm sorry. But I'm here now."

She had barely recovered from her mother's passing when she had learned of her close childhood friend's fatal mission in Afghanistan. He hadn't had the choice to come home, and she hadn't wanted to, either.

The stranger was still off to the side, examining Madison's fellow passengers unaffectedly, broad shoulders filling the space around him with pronounced author-ity. Her father turned to him.

"Briggs. Come and meet my daughter."

The man stepped closer, and Madison was aware of startlingly blue eyes study-ing her. "Nice to meet you, Miss Burke."

She took his offered hand. *Strong.* That was the first word this man brought to mind. Veins stood out on his exposed fore-arm beneath a light dusting of hair. His skin was already tanned, even so early in the spring.

"Just call me Madison." She smiled, using the charm that got interviewees to open up to her in great detail. He seemed unfazed.

She looked questioningly at her father. Why was this man here?

He read her question astutely. "Briggs Thorpe has taken over the Whitson ranch, darlin'. He will eventually own it." Her father's explanation was short, and he seemed to understand she needed more information. "I'm not supposed to drive until the doctors can run more tests, so he offered to bring me to meet you."

"What? The doctors advised you not to drive? And I don't understand. You aren't the Whitsons' foreman anymore?" Madison looked from her father to Briggs and then back again.

"That's not what I meant. It's not like that. I'm still the foreman. What I mean is, he's taken over ownership of the ranch for the Whitson family. And as for the seriousness of the situation, that's still to be determined. The doctors haven't cleared me to go back to working on the ranch just yet." Her father's face took on a melancholy expression.

"Are you saying the Whitson family sold the ranch?" Madison was still confused. "What happened?"

He held his hands up to stop her questions. "No, not exactly. Look, I'll tell you the whole story once we get out of this crowded airport. Get your bags and let's get going."

Her father looked like he was dreading

the task of telling her almost as much as he hated being in the crowded city, so Madison just nodded and went to the baggage claim for her suitcase. He would be more likely to talk when he felt more at ease.

Before she could return to where the men stood, however, her senses came alive with awareness. A faint prickling sensation along the nape of her neck shattered her illusions that the danger had been left in Boston.

Someone was watching her again.

"Get down!" Briggs yelled.

Madison was aware of strong arms wrapping around her and a sturdy chest breaking her fall as Briggs rolled with her onto the ground. In an instant, he had covered her frame with his own much larger one and drawn a gun she hadn't noticed until now from his waistband. She couldn't help thinking it was odd he had one since they were in an airport.

She didn't have time to ponder the thought further. Her attention returned to the reason he had drawn the gun. There was shouting, and security rushed toward the section of the building Briggs had aimed at. Had shots been fired? She wasn't sure, but she thought so based on Briggs's reaction.

There was an all-black-clad figure running away, a high-powered rifle with a scope dangling from one arm. The chaos around her was overwhelming. She fought the urge to shrink into a ball.

Briggs helped Madison to her feet and grasped her hand, almost dragging her across the airport.

"Wait! My father!" She was gasping, everything happening too fast.

"We aren't leaving him. I made sure he got to cover as soon as I got a chance to look up, but I have to get you out of range. The laser beam was on *your* head." Briggs tossed the reply over a very muscled shoulder as he tugged her along at a run. Shock and fear coursed through her. His reply hadn't especially reassured her about her father.

She tried to protest, but Briggs set a relentless pace, not easing up the pressure. He finally slowed as they reached a heavy door. He opened it and pulled her inside. It was little more than a supply closet, but it provided cover and a good hiding place.

He was already on the phone as her spinning thoughts settled onto what had just happened. "What are you doing?"

He looked at her like she wasn't thinking clearly. "Calling to see if it's clear. It's not safe to get you out of here until the place is secure. And they need to know you were the target."

She blew out a breath. "Who is bold enough to try to bring a gun into an airport these days?"

He spoke into the phone, then disconnected and focused on her. His eyes had narrowed to slits, and his brows set at odd angles to one another. "I have all the proper permits to carry the Glock. And I have good reason."

She felt the heat of embarrassment washing over her face when she realized he thought she was referring to him. "No,

I meant the person with the rifle." Her thoughts were still churning. "But why *do* you have the gun?"

"It's not important right now. Just know it's perfectly legal." He spoke briefly into the phone and listened, nodding as he looked at Madison. "Clear."

She nodded. "Can we check on my dad?"

Briggs eased into the corridor, taking extra precaution before turning back to her. "The shooter's long gone. Security is everywhere now."

He helped her from the closet, calling her father on his cell phone. She noticed he was careful to watch and keep her shielded as they walked quickly to the exit.

Madison felt like her whole world had just slid off its axis and hurtled through space.

Briggs kept a close watch when he and Madison met back up with Jake near baggage claim. A security officer stood close to Jake, and they were chatting like old friends. Jake had a tendency to win people over easily like that.

Briggs crossed his arms as he watched Madison wrap hers around her father in the middle of the airport terminal. She was talking to Jake in rushed sentences, and he felt like an outsider once again. It was a common occurrence for him.

He studied the pair, realizing she had him off-kilter already. She was beautiful, but that wasn't what bothered him most. She had a nervous, hunted look about her that made him immediately want to protect her. But it also made him suspicious. Why had she come here after so many years away? Was it really just her father's illness? Something about her body language had made him wonder what she was hiding even before the laser had singled her out as a target. If he had learned anything during his time in the SEALs, it was that he had a knack for reading people.

But that wasn't something he wanted to think about now. Right now, he wanted to corner Madison and demand answers from her. Why wasn't Jake demanding answers himself? Shouldn't he be more concerned? Or did he know something Briggs didn't?

The last thing Briggs wanted was trouble, and Madison seemed to have brought it right to his door. He was trying valiantly to get his life together again. In his experience, a woman could complicate things, even one who wasn't being shot at. He hadn't had the heart to deny Jake the visit from his daughter, as long as that visit remained temporary. As soon as he got a chance to speak with Madison alone, he aimed to find out what she was hiding, though.

They settled into his red GMC dually and started out of the city. Jake had insisted Madison ride in the passenger seat. Briggs navigated the busy freeways, noticing the surreptitious glances she gave him. Honestly, he had felt a little bad about studying her when they'd first met, and had tried not to make her uncomfortable when he had realized what he was doing. He had seen enough, though.

She was definitely attractive. Her long hair was chestnut brown with some red streaks that caught the light. She wore slightly baggy clothes that made it difficult to tell much about her build, but he knew she wasn't overly tall. She was just right in height and build.

Much like Emily had been.

Madison broke into his thoughts when she turned her attention away from her father and spoke his name. "Mr. Thorpe, are you originally from Oklahoma?"

"Briggs." He corrected her almost automatically. No one called him Mr. Thorpe, not even the hands at the ranch. "I'm from Wyoming. Born and raised."

"Ah." She didn't say anything else for a long moment. Maybe she thought he would elaborate. He wouldn't. He wasn't at all sure how she was so easily making small talk after what had just happened. Maybe it was her way of dealing with the shock.

"How do you know Zeke and Miranda Whitson?" She had clearly waited as long as she could.

Uh-oh.

He cleared his throat. "I served in the navy with their son."

His chest seized up at the thought of the questions that would come next. He took slow, deep breaths. How could he discourage her? He didn't have the capacity to talk about Wade with a stranger.

"You knew Wade." She surprised him with the quiet statement.

Wade had been the Whitsons' son. Their only child.

He looked at her from the corner of his eye. "*You* knew Wade? I thought he left before your father started working for the Whitson family."

"Of course I knew Wade. We lived in the same small town, grew up together and became friends when we were young, long before Dad took the job at their ranch." She didn't say any more, and Briggs was left wondering what she knew about how Wade died. The thought hurt too much to ponder, so he pushed it away. He definitely wasn't going to ask her.

She certainly seemed less nervous after leaving the airport, but he noticed she kept looking behind them, as if she expected them to be followed or something. Honestly, he had the same suspicions and kept watching for a tail as well.

Whoever had aimed that rifle at Madison wasn't a random shooter, and Briggs didn't think he would give up easily. And of course, since the shooter had gotten away, they could be anywhere. Instinct kept his own awareness high, along with practiced caution from experience, but he noticed nothing unusual other than her behavior.

He finally just asked the questions that were weighing on his mind. "Do you know why someone might be trying to kill you?"

Her eyes widened for a split second. She glanced back at Jake. He was mostly just taking in the conversation with concern on his face. He seemed to be in shock. Maybe he felt Briggs was doing a fine job asking the questions. "No. No, I don't. So you don't think it was a random shooter?"

He almost wanted to roll his eyes. She wasn't very good at lying. He knew she didn't for a second believe it was random, either. "It didn't look like they were aiming that rifle at anyone else."

Madison shrugged. "I guess not."

"You know more than you're letting on." His accusatory tone rang loud in the cab of the truck.

"Madison, talk to us, honey. We want to help." Her father had to lean forward a bit to hear her responses, and now he was scooting as far as his seatbelt would allow.

Madison paled. "I don't know anything. Really. If I did, I would admit it, but I don't know who might want me dead."

She shuddered, and he felt a surge of sympathy for her. He might be used to a life of violence and survival, but she clearly was not. He would be more likely to get answers from her if he eased up and gave her some space for the moment.

They rode in silence for a while, until she finally opened up. "I don't know for sure that it's related, but I was attacked a couple of nights ago in Boston. I have no idea why. The police thought I was just a random victim. I wasn't so sure, but I had no evidence."

Briggs didn't reply for a few beats, but he finally addressed her comment. "What makes you say that?"

She sighed. "I know it sounds silly, but I feel like someone has been watching me." She didn't say anything more for a moment.

"For how long?" Briggs asked.

She cut her gaze to the window. "I don't know. A couple of weeks? It's just a gut feeling I have."

Briggs's jaw twitched. "I'd say you're probably right, considering what happened back there at the airport. I wouldn't go anywhere alone for a while if I were you."

She nodded slowly. "I don't want to, anyway."

He thought there was a hint of guilt in her voice, as if she was worried it was too much for her father. Was that just his imagination?

The cab was silent for a little while before Madison finally changed the subject. "I haven't been on the ranch in a long time. I wonder how much has changed."

He grinned and glanced at the rearview mirror. "We won't ask you to herd the buffalo while you visit. You won't have to worry about your riding skills or anything."

She shook her head. "I might have moved to the city, but I'm sure I can still ride. Is the buffalo herd growing? The Whitsons were having a rough year the last time I was here."

Briggs noticed she turned and animatedly encouraged her father when he began to answer, filling her in on the latest developments from the back seat. Briggs didn't intentionally tune their conversation out, but his thoughts were on other things. Like what was going on with Madison Burke, and why she had become a target.

When her stare lasered in on him, he realized she had asked him a question directly. He tried for a vague response, seeing as he had only heard bits and pieces of the conversation. "Yeah, we've made some improvements. But—"

Her odd expression said he had gotten it wrong, but her phone chimed, interrupting the conversation. She frowned at it.

"Is everything okay?" Briggs asked. He looked at Jake in the rearview mirror and saw the same concern he felt reflected in Jake's wizened face.

"Um, yeah, I think so. It's my friend Adria." She silenced the device and slid it into an expensive-looking leather handbag.

Briggs wondered why her demeanor had changed if it was just a simple text from a friend. Maybe her friend had learned something. He didn't get a chance to find out before she changed the subject again.

"Wade and I used to feed the orphaned calves together." She made the statement into the tense silence. "Our mothers were close friends, so we became as close as brother and sister growing up." She was looking to distract them, to change the course of the conversation. Briggs didn't like how much anxiety being a target was causing her, but until he could get more details from her, he didn't know what to do about it. He didn't do much to help with his noncommittal replies. He couldn't bring himself to talk about Wade. Soon she was on another subject with her father.

Madison continued to chatter nervously with Jake almost the whole way to the ranch, and Briggs tuned most of it out. His thoughts were consumed with her predicament. As much as he wanted to just send her back to Boston and not worry about it, he knew he couldn't do that. Jake had been good to him, and Madison was clearly the old man's whole reason for existence, despite her long absence. He had never seen the crusty foreman light up the way he had when he'd found out Madison was coming to see him.

When they reached the ranch house, Briggs grabbed her suitcase from the back seat of the truck and started for the porch.

"Where are you going?" Madison's voice was close behind him. He turned to look at her and found she had gone completely white.

"To the guest room? I'm gentleman enough not to expect you to sleep on the sofa in the barn loft." Briggs almost growled the words out. He felt badly enough that Jake wouldn't accept better living arrangements, anyway, and he sure wouldn't send Madison to the tiny loft apartment.

According to Jake, the Burkes had lived on their own small operation when Madison was growing up, a tiny sixty-acre ranch where they kept horses and some show cattle and such. But Jake had sold it after his wife's death to pay off the medical bills. The cost of the cancer treatments had eaten away at their life's savings, and as a single man, he had no longer needed the space. Jake had requested the barn loft as his living quarters as part of his salary.

"Oh, it's fine. I can stay in the barn." Madison was still speaking when Jake began shaking his head.

"No, ma'am. It's a terrible sofa and one tiny bed, and I don't aim to give up the bed for ya at my age. You stay in the house. Briggs'll be a perfect gentleman, I can promise you. Besides, I think you'll be safer here." He gestured toward the house.

Briggs chuckled and nodded. "Jake should stay in the house while you visit also, especially if that makes you feel better. I've been trying to get him to quit climbing the stairs to that barn loft, anyway. There's plenty of room in the house."

"Well." Madison stood there looking them over for a moment, clearly uncomfortable. "If you're sure. I don't want to intrude."

Jake adjusted his hat. "I'll just go grab some of my things, then."

Madison took a moment to respond. She sucked in a long breath as though gathering her courage. He thought she might even be trembling a little. In the end, she relented, and he led the way to the guest room and set her luggage inside. She thanked him and seemed to be waiting for his departure. When he stood there a moment too long, her smile faded. She began to look around nervously, taking in her surroundings. He could read her expression almost as clearly as if she had spoken her thoughts aloud.

It was the first time she had been here since Wade had passed. No doubt the house was full of memories for her. Her heart was surely twisting in her chest at the thought.

She tried for distraction. "I haven't talked to my dad much until recently."

"He said you'd had a falling out. I'm glad you're getting things straightened out between you." Briggs led the way back to the living room and offered her a seat.

She still looked nervous. "He never explained about the Whitsons. What happened? He told me Zeke passed away, but he didn't mention the ranch having a new owner. Why did you take over?"

He noticed she was looking around the house, especially down the hall toward Wade's old room. This had to be hard for her. His answer wouldn't make it any easier, but she deserved a response.

"They didn't sell. Zeke died of a heart attack six months ago. And Miranda…is in a long-term care facility. She had a pretty severe stroke not long after. I'm running the place for her. She wants to leave it to me." Briggs tried to keep his voice steady. It didn't work.

"Ah." She blinked and turned away. "Wade was supposed to take over, but he never came home. I still can't believe he's gone."

Her soft response was full of grief. His chest ached for her.

"Yeah. So I came… I came to visit his parents and it fell to me." He straightened and pierced her with a direct look. "Wade was my closest friend in the SEALs. I felt like I owe his parents something. What else could I do?"

He hated the sympathy that filled her eyes. He didn't want that to be her first impression of him, but somehow knowing she felt Wade's loss as well made it easier.

"Wade was a good guy. We grew apart as we got older, but there was always that bond. At least, that's how it was for me.

Maybe it was different for Wade. He always called me Chop, but that's a whole other story."

A jolt of surprise hit Briggs then. Wade had shared tons of stories about scrapes he had gotten into with Chop, but he had never suspected Chop was a girl. Wade had never let on. It gave him way more insight into Madison's personality than she probably would've liked for him to have.

"Chop, huh? There has to be a pretty good story behind that nickname." He couldn't hold back his grin.

She turned adorably pink, and he tried to remind himself not to find it so intriguing. "Yeah. I'll do my best to distract you from hearing about that one."

"First things first, though." Briggs frowned at her. "It's obvious that you're in some pretty serious danger. I need you to tell me every last detail."

He paused, and she hesitated. He knew she felt far too many emotions right now, not least of all fear. It hadn't left her since the airport. She seemed hesitant to confide in him about what was happening, and he needed to know as soon as possible in order to protect her. If he had to use that fear to his advantage right now to be better prepared, then so be it. He would do what he had to do. No way would he see another woman come to the same fate as his former fiancée.

He pushed Emily from his mind. He couldn't dwell on his loss now.

He drew in a deep breath, knowing this was likely going to be hard on them both, but he had to know what he was dealing with here. She looked at him with wide eyes as he cleared his throat.

"Madison, tell me everything. Your life might depend on it."

TWO

Madison backed away.

How had this complete stranger read her so easily? She was hedging a little, true, but mostly to try to gather her wits. This whole set of circumstances had her shaken.

Standing in his former home, she felt Wade's absence acutely. Memories were everywhere. Echoes of his voice and his laughter haunted her from every room. She was overcome with a bitter ache brought on by all the reminders that Wade was gone too soon. And now Wade's dad, with his deep voice and ready smile, was gone as well. It was too much.

She forced the thoughts and memories to the shadows of her mind and refocused on Briggs. What had him so upset by all this? Her instincts told her it went deeper than keeping a stranger safe.

His blue eyes blazed, burning into her own. His words had replaced her grief with raw fear. *Your life might depend on it.*

She couldn't hold back a shiver. Why would anyone want her dead?

Briggs kept watching her face intently, compounding her nervousness with every heartbeat. How could she answer his questions when she couldn't figure it out herself? How could she tell a total stranger what kind of turmoil her life had just become? Especially this stranger. Not only was he one of the most handsome men she had ever seen, but there was something dependable about him that made her miss having someone there to take care of her. It was a scary feeling. She was thriving independently, wasn't she?

"I'm not trying to hide anything from you. I just really don't know what's going on." Her breathing came a little faster. She set her carry-on case on a nearby chair and pulled out her computer.

"What are you doing?"

"It will be easier just to show you." She opened the email and displayed the videos she had received as she boarded the flight to Oklahoma.

His eyes widened as he realized what he was looking at. "Is this your apartment?"

"Yes. I received this just as I got on the plane." She pulled up the email with the attached videos of her apartment.

His face darkened into a frightening scowl. "Have you reported this?"

"Only to my boss at work. He promised to notify the authorities in Boston." She wrapped her arms around her own waist.

"In Boston? I think you need to report it here. Never mind, I'll see to it myself. Someone was just shooting at you. I know you don't have any reason to trust me, but maybe I can help." His focused gaze made her even more on edge.

"You're right. I don't know you. And I don't want to burden you with my problems. It's nothing I can't take care of. I appreciate your kindness, though." Madison forced herself to relax.

He blew out a quick breath. Was she frustrating him? It couldn't be helped. He looked at her for a long moment before speaking again.

"You know, Madison. I know a thing or two about protecting people."

She expected him to continue, but he never did.

At that moment, she heard her father's sharply indrawn breath behind her. He was looking at the computer screen. She couldn't play the situation down now, and it would put additional strain on her dad. This was why she hadn't wanted to talk about it. He had enough to deal with considering his declining health. The stress of someone targeting her wouldn't help his condition at all.

"Is this the only email you've received?" Briggs was looking at the screen again.

"Yes. I told you about the attack in Boston. I've been a little frightened ever since. I started feeling like I was being watched everywhere I went. I never saw anyone watching me, but I could feel it." She tightened her arms around herself to ease the shuddering. Now that she began to talk about it, the words tumbled out.

Briggs's eyes had darkened. "And then someone started shooting at you at the airport. Did your father know about this before you came?"

He glanced at Jake, and she was sure the answer was obvious. Her father looked completely shell-shocked.

She shook her head. "I didn't want to worry him. I just wanted to see him, spend some quality time with him, make sure he gets the proper care. This isn't why I came. I give you my word. I came because of my father's illness."

Jake cleared his throat behind her. "I wish you would have told me."

Briggs nodded his agreement and pulled out his cell phone. "Well, I'm glad you're here."

"What are you doing?" She could see

he was obviously making a call. But why? And to whom?

"I'm going to report this to the local sheriff. Then I'm going to call my brother. I'll explain in a moment."

She tapped a toe as she waited for him to finish his call out in the hall. Why would he call his brother? Her father stood silently as well.

When Briggs finally finished his conversation, he reentered the room. "My baby brother, Avery, is a private detective. He's going to look into it."

Madison felt her face flame. "You— But— I didn't ask you to do that."

"Don't worry. He's doing it as a favor to me. It won't cost you anything." Briggs tucked his phone into the back pocket of his jeans. "It's the least I can do. Your father has been my saving grace since I arrived at the ranch."

"Oh. Is it really necessary, though?" Hot tears gathered behind her eyes. This was all just too much. She sat down on a chair by the window.

His expression was sympathetic. "This isn't something to take chances with, Madison. You could be in real danger here. The sooner we catch the culprit, the better."

Madison squeezed her eyes closed for a moment and took a deep breath. She knew he only wanted to help, but she felt awful about this. She just wanted it to all go away. "Maybe so. I'm sorry to be so much trouble. It wasn't my intention."

Briggs stepped closer to her. "No worries. I'm glad to help."

Her father finally spoke up from just behind her. "I don't want you to go back to Boston until I at least know you're safe."

She started to reply that she couldn't stay here forever, but the look Briggs wore stopped her. He wouldn't accept her refusal.

Madison admitted temporary defeat.

"I guess you're right." She plopped back in the chair, too weary to do anything else.

"Is that all? That's everything you know?" Briggs waited patiently.

She thought for a moment, then scrolled

through her phone. "As I told you, I contacted my boss at the newspaper when I was on the plane, and the text I received in the truck earlier was from my friend and coworker, Adria. She told me that my supervisor, Davis, forwarded the information to the police. Investigators went to my apartment to look it over and found there were six cameras in total."

"How many rooms are in your apartment?" Brings asked the question with a furrowed brow.

"Only four. It's a one-bedroom. There was at least one in every room. Two in the living room and two in the kitchen."

The knowledge that someone had been watching her every move in the privacy of her own home made her sick to her stomach. She couldn't look at her father or Briggs, knowing they were probably thinking the same thing.

"What are they going to do about it?" her father asked.

"I don't know. She just said they found the cameras and she would let me know when she knew more." Madison averted her eyes.

"Avery would probably get you some information sooner. If you'll let me, I'll see what he can do," Briggs said.

She glanced up at him but then quickly looked away again. "Why? None of this makes any sense to me."

Briggs was silent for a moment. "I don't know, but we will figure it out. And this isn't your fault, you know. You have nothing to be embarrassed about."

"What if it is?" Her voice was small. She finally looked at him—really *looked* at him.

"How could it be your fault?" Briggs asked.

"Maybe someone didn't like something I wrote. Maybe I should have been more careful." She shrugged. "Maybe this is how they plan to get back at me. They want to make me feel scrutinized because I made their life public or something."

"Do you always write the truth?" Briggs asked.

"Of course." She looked at him question-ingly. What was he getting at?

"Then you've almost certainly offended someone. But that's on them, not you. They should have behaved better. I'll have Avery look into your recent stories and people who might have been connected to them." Briggs went toward the door. "Until we know more, don't go anywhere alone."

Jake nodded in agreement. "Promise me you won't leave the house without telling someone."

"I promise. I really don't want to be a burden, though." Madison bit her lower lip.

"You won't be as long as you stay with someone until we get this figured out. I need to go take care of some things in the barn, but I'll check in with your father as soon as I return. Just keep one of us close, okay?" Briggs left the room, his face set in a strong, determined expression.

She had the feeling he had stepped back into his days in the navy and was suddenly curious about what his life had been like as a SEAL. What had made him want to be one of the toughest soldiers on the planet? And why wasn't he still in the SEALs?

She would find out before she left. The question that nagged at her most relentlessly, however, was why she was so intrigued by Briggs Thorpe. She didn't want any more men in her life. Her thoughts were in a jumble, but she knew she didn't want a repeat of the past. It made her cautious about even thinking of romantic relationships. Her former fiancé had nearly ruined her life, and she had almost let him. Her judgment was not to be trusted when it came to men. She needed to remember that.

Briggs tried holding his breath. He counted. He did all he could to refocus his mind. Distract himself.

But he was still angry.

The idea that someone had so brutally invaded Madison's privacy was gut-wrenching. He couldn't imagine how violated she must feel knowing someone had been watching all the most intimate moments of

her life. And for what? Was someone trying to learn her habits to figure out how
best to kill her, or were they just terror-
izing her before they killed her? Was this
about revenge? A fascination with her of
some sort? It seemed certain this person
wanted her dead. But why?

The evil of it all sickened him. As a
SEAL, he'd stared evil in the face, but this
was a different sort of disturbing. He didn't
want to consider why, since he was pretty
sure it had a little too much to do with the
intriguing brunette beauty involved. And
his past didn't help.

He had left some documents in the barn
and wanted to retrieve them now, mostly
to give his anger time to cool. The grants
for the buffalo, or American bison, would
need to be renewed soon. The grants were
what kept the ranch afloat, with the way
modern farming was going. Restoring the
population of the historic animals had become national interest, and he was manag-
ing one of the best herds around, thanks to
Zeke and Miranda Whitson. He couldn't

falter with their legacy. Even now, in the long-term care facility, Miranda was passionate about the buffalo.

He could relate to that kind of passion. It was what had led him to become a SEAL—to become the best defender he could be. He had a strong desire to protect innocent people and defend their freedom.

And he wanted to make up for his past failings.

Briggs wasn't sure why he was so protective of Madison in particular after such a short period of time, but he couldn't deny he felt this on a deeply personal level. True, her father had been invaluable since he took over the Whitson Ranch, but the loyal foreman alone wasn't enough to inspire such concern for her safety. If he considered it closely, Madison herself was the cause. She looked independent, self-sufficient and in control, but something behind her eyes hinted at a struggle with her past. That he could relate to.

Briggs returned through the back door a little while later to find Madison and

Jake sitting at the farmhouse table in the kitchen, deep in conversation. She rose when he entered.

"Would you like some coffee? Mrs. Newman was kind enough to make us a fresh pot." Madison was already on her way to get him a cup.

Mrs. Newman, a widow who did the cooking and domestic care of the home, was the only other woman on the place. She had her own home a short distance from the ranch, but she spent long hours on the ranch taking care of the men's meals and such. There were a lot of them to feed and clean up after.

He started to refuse, but maybe keeping busy would help Madison right now. "Thank you. Coffee would be nice. Just black."

Madison nodded and poured him a cup. He didn't know how to feel about the way she was so comfortable in his kitchen already. Mrs. Newman must've shown her where to find things, but he was a little shaken at how natural she looked there.

Maybe it had to do with his recent thoughts about protecting her. Or maybe he had been out of a relationship for too long.

He shook off the thought and accepted the warm mug. He was happy alone. "I won't intrude on your visit. I have some business to take care of in my office."

"Briggs, stay." Jake stopped him, an outstretched hand emphasizing his wish.

Briggs furrowed his brow but pulled up a chair. "You wanna talk about something?"

Jake hesitated. "Madison wants to catch an early flight home in the morning. She's...uncomfortable staying right now. She thinks she's being a burden and putting us in danger needlessly."

Briggs thought that was about the most backward thing he had ever heard. Shouldn't she be hoping to stay *longer*? At least until they could figure this out? "Why? Have I made you feel unwelcome?"

She looked shocked at his direct question. "Of course not. I just don't want to put you or my father in any danger. And I have pets at my apartment that a friend has been caring for. I don't want to endanger her, either. It just makes sense to return and figure this all out."

"It doesn't make sense to me." Briggs set his cup on the table with a loud thump. "Your father and I are grown men. And the police can figure it out just fine with minimal help from you."

She actually laughed. It made his insides soft and warm, which had Briggs rethinking his decision. Maybe it would be best to send her away. He didn't need a woman getting him all emotional. But that wasn't who he was.

"See if your friend can take your pets to her place. I can't let you leave here not knowing if you'll get back to Boston safely or not. I'm a retired navy SEAL. I can take care of your father and myself."

She looked a little relieved at first, but then her face colored. Was she embarrassed or angry at his taking charge?

"I hardly know you. It feels like an imposition." She looked at her father, who was shaking his head.

"I wouldn't offer to have you stay if it were." Briggs had no intention of arguing further. "This is no longer up for debate. You are staying here."

Jake's already gray pallor went lighter. "He's right, honey. You need protection, and this is the best way. I couldn't rest if I didn't know you were safe."

Madison swallowed. Was that relief he saw in her eyes? "It appears I'm outnumbered."

Briggs nodded. "Then it's settled. I'm taking some calves to the stockyards early in the morning. You'd better ride with me." He put his coffee cup to his lips, hoping she didn't argue again. "The county sheriff is sending extra patrols out this way to help keep an eye out for any strange activity. They haven't found anything else that could pinpoint the shooter at the airport, though. Whoever it was is still out there, and they are sure to try again."

A heartbeat passed while she tried to absorb what he had just said. She finally seemed to soften.

"All right. And thank you. I appreciate how good you've been to my father, and now to me. Thank you for opening your home." Madison smiled at him, and he nearly choked on his coffee. Good thing he knew how to practically overcome drowning.

He might be a former SEAL, but this could turn out to be one of his toughest assignments yet, self-appointed or not.

In fact, he was almost certain of it.

THREE

Madison was a little groggy in the morning when Briggs came into the house to tell her it was time to go. She was nursing a too-hot mug of coffee, taking tiny sips and hoping enough caffeine would penetrate the fog to get her moving.

The night before, she had stayed up late talking to her father after dinner and found she had missed him so much more than she had thought. Before her mother died, her father had told her she wasn't needed around here anymore, and she should just go on to the city and get on with her life.

The diagnosis had been terminal cancer, but doctors planned extensive treatment and expected her to live for another year or two. Madison had carried on with her life, too busy to spend much time with her mother. But the cancer had taken hold quicker than they had expected, and her mother passed away before Madison came to grips with the situation.

She had failed to resolve small issues between her and her mother. Shame and embarrassment had kept her away more than anything after that. She had felt selfish for not dropping her own agenda to spend more time with her mother while she was alive.

By the time they had the funeral, her father was angry with her for her behavior and wasn't speaking to her. She had been hurt by his easy dismissal of her from his life but realized now he had just been hurting. He probably hadn't wanted her to see his pain or cause her more pain. He'd dealt with it the only way he knew how, and she had responded like a spoiled child, refusing to talk to him about the grief and loss they were both going through.

Her father's soothing words from last night had put some of her worries about it to rest, and though she still hadn't quite forgiven herself, it helped to know her father wasn't upset with her about it. She thought she could begin to forgive herself and move forward now.

Her father had, however, chastised her for not coming to him sooner about the strange things that had been happening. Now there were threats on her life, and though it might not have solved anything, he felt she should have told someone sooner. Truthfully, she was terribly frightened, but she was grateful she now had someone else to help her deal with the situation.

Briggs led her outside to the truck. A thirty-two-foot stock trailer squatted behind it, loaded down with yearling calves. Aside from the buffalo that the ranch specialized in, they also raised some commercial cattle to supplement the income and keep the place profitable.

Briggs waited for her to pass and then held the truck door open while she climbed into the passenger seat. He didn't say much, just got behind the wheel, blue eyes glowing bright in the early morning sun. Maybe he wasn't the talkative sort in the morning. That was fine with her since she really wasn't, either.

She was surprised at how good it felt to be back here. Not just with her dad, but in Oklahoma, where life moved slower. The spaces were wide open, and the sun shone in golden rays over the misty grasses of the morning. It was soothing to her country-girl soul, and she wanted to breathe it in deeply, to take in the scent of spring grasses and the freshness of a dewy morning.

She had missed this land more than she thought.

There was such hope present in a sunny spring morning in the country. She couldn't help feeling she belonged here, with the swaying oaks and gently rolling hills. She was at peace just from her surroundings, and all seemed right with the world, especially since things seemed to be better with her father. He had assured her he had no hard feelings and that he was just happy to have her here. She felt as if a weight had been shed from her very being.

As she and Briggs drove away from the ranch house, she watched the buffalo graze peacefully in a nearby pasture, their furry chocolate-brown coats blowing in the breeze. The massive creatures in the grassy field were a pastoral picture from the past, and she couldn't help wondering if this herd looked the same as their ancestors had over a century before when the human population was scarce and the bison had no worries.

The ranch driveway wound out to a paved two-lane highway that led through more pastureland and farms, a picture of serene country beauty.

It didn't stay peaceful for long, though. Briggs kept his eyes on the road, but when he spoke, Madison knew from the tension in the cab that something was up.

"Madison. Don't panic, but I want you to be prepared. There is an SUV gaining on us too fast from behind. I don't know

what their plan is, but it doesn't look good."
Briggs was stone-cold calm.

"Like, following us?" Her own voice
rose an octave.

"Yeah, at the very least. This isn't going
to be easy with a loaded stock trailer. I'm
going to try to find a place to pull over and
see if they will just go on around. I'm not
sure what they will do if that's not what
they want. Get ready to call 911 just in
case." Briggs was watching his mirrors as
he spoke, still sounding perfectly calm.

It was almost maddening.

There was a small area ahead where the
shoulder widened into a large, flat gravel
surface, and Briggs slowed to ease his way
over. However, before he could do so, the
large SUV sped up and came around beside the truck. She couldn't tell much about
the driver other than they had a small
frame. A ball cap and bandanna covered
the person's identity. Before she could note
anything else, the SUV rammed into the
driver's side of the truck, sending it skid-
ding sideways toward the ditch.

Madison barely held back a scream.

Briggs recovered control smoothly, though the trailer fishtailed a bit before he could steady it. The SUV slammed into them again, and this time, the trailer began to shimmy and shake around the road. The SUV fell back. The rig was still moving quickly enough to make it hard to control, and Briggs's grip visibly tightened on the wheel. His knuckles turned white at the joints as he tried to slow the rig down at a gradual pace. It felt counterintuitive, but she knew it wasn't safe to keep up the faster pace. Besides, there was no way he could outrun the SUV while towing a trailer full of calves, anyway.

Madison fought the urge to cry out as the SUV approached again.

"Might wanna go ahead and call 911 now." Briggs gritted the reminder out through tight lips. Glad for the distraction of having something to occupy her, Madison shook off her stupor to do as he asked, digging for the phone in her handbag. She thought there might be a hint of humor in his tone, though. Was he laughing at her for freezing in horror? Was he really finding amusement in her reaction at a time like this?

"I'm sorry. I didn't think." She pressed the buttons on her phone to place the call, flinching as the SUV sped up and skidded into them again. This time, the trailer wheels caught on some loose gravel along the shoulder, throwing the whole rig off balance and hurtling them into the ditch.

Madison heard her own shriek as if from afar. Her head struck something solid as the trailer began to roll sideways with the heavy weight of the calves, pulling the truck along with it. Thudding and bawling filled the air as the calves slid and tumbled to one side of the stock trailer, creating more momentum for the trailer to roll and rock harder before finally settling on one side amid dust and debris. There was a jolt of the truck rocking as well before everything at last went still.

* * *

Briggs took a deep breath and assessed the situation.

Madison had been slammed against the passenger side door, and from the look of the cracked glass, she had hit her head on the window. He barely noticed his own injuries as the rig came to a standstill on its side. Diesel exhaust and the musty scent of the cattle filled the air of the cab.

Tires screeched again, and the SUV made a U-turn, coming back toward the overturned rig. Gunshots rang out as the vehicle came nearer. Someone in the SUV was shooting at them from the slightly lowered window. They were dangling almost upside down, though, so it was difficult for the perpetrator to get off a clean shot.

Briggs motioned for Madison to stay low in the cab of the truck as the metallic ping of bullets against the frame rang out sporadically.

The sound of another vehicle's approach sent the SUV speeding away, giving Briggs and Madison a chance to breathe again.

Briggs reached for the seat belt that held him trapped against the sideways truck seat. He held on to the roof's handle near his head so he wouldn't tumble into Madison as the seat belt gave way.

"Are you okay?" Briggs slid down the seat slowly, using the steering wheel as help for control.

Madison was rubbing the side of her head. He could imagine a knot was already forming if she had hit the glass as he assumed she had. A trickle of blood oozed down her hand where she had touched it. Probably split open. "Yes, just a bump on the head, I think. How about you?"

Briggs shook his head. "I'm fine. But you have more than a bump. It's bleeding pretty good." He handed her a clean rag he pulled from the glove box. "Keep some pressure on it. When we get out of here, will you call to report the accident while I check on the calves? We need to get some help on the way just in case that SUV decides to come back."

She nodded, and he moved back toward the driver's side door over his head, wrenching it open and hoisting himself out the skyward-facing door. He balanced on the side of the truck a moment and then stretched out a hand toward her.

"Can you climb out?" He looked over his shoulder once more, curious about the other vehicle approaching and verifying their attacker was actually gone.

Madison hesitated for a moment, probably trying to find another way out of the truck's cab. There was none, though, so she stood up against the passenger side door and struggled a moment to pull herself up and free of the truck's cab. Once they were both out, Briggs helped her to the ground, where he looked her over once more to be sure she didn't have any other injuries.

"I really am fine." Madison was watching him, and he thought she sounded a little amused.

Briggs nodded, satisfied, and walked around the truck.

He heard Madison calling in the accident while he was looking over the mess of bawling calves in the overturned trailer. The sides on the stock trailer were enclosed most of the way up, vented only on the top one-third. To his relief, it kept the calves that were struggling to their feet again from getting their legs stuck in the wide cracks. Panicked calves and broken legs would only compound his problems. Most had managed to regain their footing against the solid portion of the side, and all appeared to be okay, for the most part. They were far from calm, however, jumping and shoving against one another in frantic efforts to escape.

Briggs spoke softly to the calves, trying to calm them.

"Oh, they're pitiful." Madison joined Briggs beside the trailer. She, too, began to speak to the calves sweetly, her soft voice gently soothing.

The approaching vehicle drew their attention. Briggs wanted to reassure her, but he really had nothing to offer her at the moment. He was also worried the driver of the SUV might yet come back to finish the job, but it was a familiar truck that slowed on the road beside them. Briggs recognized fellow rancher Seth Akins in the cab of the dually.

"Everyone okay?" Seth took in the scene, from Briggs and Madison, to the overturned truck and trailer and calves. He eyed Madison's head before glancing back at Briggs.

"Thanks for stopping, Seth. We're fine. We've called for help. Someone intentionally ran us off the road."

Seth's eyes widened.

"What? Wow. Did you get a tag number or anything? I can call my cousin at the sheriff's department." Seth reached for his cell phone.

"There was no tag. It was a dark SUV with heavily tinted windows. Should have some pretty decent-sized dents and scratches, though, considering the repeated impacts with my truck. He had to have picked up some red paint." Briggs looked back at the bawling calves. "It's a wonder none of these guys are badly injured. We have a bit of a dilemma, though. Getting these calves out and righting the trailer might be tough."

Briggs noticed Madison was still watching the road, but the plight of the calves seemed to weigh heavily on her as well. "So, how will this work? You have to right the trailer, but if you turn the calves out, they'll be in the highway," Madison said as she assessed their surroundings. The highway wasn't terribly busy, but there were still occasional cars passing by.

Briggs pressed his lips together. "We might have to transfer them to another trailer." He studied the calves. "If we open the doors on the new trailer, back up close enough to this one that they can't squeeze out, and herd them into the empty trailer, maybe we'll keep from losing any of them."

"I can go get my trailer, if you wanna give it a try." Seth made the offer as he adjusted the ball cap on the curls covering his blond head.

Briggs nodded. "That would be great, if you don't mind."

Seth shook his head. "Not at all. I know you'd do the same. Be right back."

He shifted his truck into gear and disappeared while Briggs and Madison continued to soothe the bawling calves. By the time emergency personnel arrived, the calves had settled a bit. Briggs couldn't help noticing that Madison was actually really good with them.

The highway patrol approached, interrupting his thoughts. The trooper pulled to the shoulder and got out of the car. He was young and looked over the truck and trailer with an expression of curious fascination, waiting until he was close to speak.

"I'm Cole Darby." He stuck out a hand toward Briggs. "There's a wrecker on the way. Any thoughts on what you wanna do about those calves?"

Briggs shook the trooper's hand and introduced himself. "A neighbor just left to get his stock trailer since he lives pretty close by. I think we have a plan to get them out."

The young officer listened intently as Briggs explained. "That sounds like it could work. We'll finish the accident report while we wait. What was the cause of the rollover?"

Briggs told the story, and the young officer took it down. Madison stood to the side, every approaching vehicle making her visibly stiffen.

"Any reason someone might intentionally force you off the road?" the officer asked.

Briggs gave Madison an apologetic glance. "Miss Burke here has had a few incidents lately. I think this might be related."

Officer Darby turned to Madison. "Miss Burke? Do you also think it's related?"

Madison was frowning. She didn't answer right away, and Briggs felt a wave of sympathy for her. "I'm not positive, but it seems likely," she finally agreed.

"Can you explain these incidents to me,

ma'am?" Officer Darby shifted his weight, still watching Madison.

Madison flushed, but she began to relay the recent events to the young officer. He listened intently, nodding here and there. By the time she finished, his mouth had turned down into a frown.

"And these incidents have been reported?" Officer Darby didn't seem convinced.

Madison nodded. "Back in Boston. I have been communicating with my boss, and he went to the Boston PD about it, but then this happened."

"Have *you* spoken to the Boston PD?" Officer Darby's comment drew a scowl from Briggs. He crossed his arms.

"No." Madison frowned. "I forwarded everything to my boss and he promised to handle it. Do you think I also need to contact them?"

"It wouldn't hurt. The county sheriff's department here will take it over, though, considering yesterday's attempted shooting and now this latest development. The case seems to be growing. How long are you here for?" Officer Darby addressed Madison with the question.

"I'm not sure now." Madison looked at Briggs. "My plans have changed. I will be staying for a while."

Briggs knew her boss wouldn't be happy to hear that, but it couldn't be helped. He nodded and took over the discussion with the officer. "Her father and I both feel that she will be safer here until we figure this out."

"Mmm-hmm." The officer made some other vague noises. "That's probably true. I'm going to call in to headquarters while we wait on your friend and let them know everything is under control. I'll be right back."

He walked away, and Briggs turned to Madison. "So, have you considered someone you work with could be behind this?"

Madison paled visibly. "I hate to think of anyone I know doing such a thing. There are some people there that I don't know well, but I have no idea why any of them would want to kill me."

He hated to be the one to shatter what peace she had left, but she needed to be aware of the danger she was in.

"I think it's definitely someone you know. Probably someone you know well."

She shivered and looked up, and her eyes widened, bringing his thoughts back to the moment. "What is it?"

She sucked in a breath. "The SUV. I think that's it over there."

FOUR

Briggs wasted no time in getting Madison behind the trailer, shielding her from the speeding SUV. He knew they might shoot from the vehicle again, but he was more concerned that they'd try to finish the job by ramming into the trailer and shoving it in their direction. What he didn't expect was the tiny explosive device that the SUV driver hurled out the window at them before speeding away.

The small metal device clinked ominously as it hit the shoulder of the road and rolled toward them. He heard Madison's gasp as recognition flooded her.

"Get down!" He yelled the command even as he took a risk he hadn't had to consider since leaving the SEALs. He ran toward the device, prodded by years of training and a sense of heroism he couldn't seem to help. Though it only took seconds to reach, the flashes of memory came to him like movie clips on a mental reel, shaking through him with shattering emotion. He saw Wade's face. He was grinning and laughing that infectious laugh of his. Screams started, echoing in his ears. He wanted to cover them as he ran, even knowing it wasn't real. He saw flashes of his team jumping into action as he gave commands.

Briggs reached the device, and without hesitation, he snatched it up and pitched it as hard as he could out into the open field just beyond them. It exploded in midair, but the flames opened up into the grass below. He saw something else, though. Not flaming grass, but Wade's form, jerking forward and falling ever so slowly as the flames glowed all around him, consuming him.

He stood there panting, remembering.

He had tried to drag Wade out. The last

thing he remembered was trying to find a way to pull Wade's fire-engulfed form out of the wreckage before his remaining men had physically disentangled Briggs and carried him away. He had fought them the whole way. The roaring he heard then was his own screams rumbling from deep in his chest.

"Briggs, are you okay?" Madison was standing beside him, lightly touching his arm, and it was evident her concern was for his mental state rather than his physical well-being. She was watching his face, his eyes.

He had to get a grip on himself. He took a deep breath, but before he could answer Madison, the young trooper was there, awe written all over his face. "That was a gutsy move. I've never seen anything like that before other than in the movies."

Briggs shook himself out of it, though it took monumental effort. "I don't recommend trying it. I served as a navy SEAL. I know from experience how long it takes for those types of explosives to detonate.

But even with that knowledge, it's still risky."

The trooper continued to gaze at him in admiration. "Whoa. That's pretty awesome."

Madison looked horrified. "It was incredibly risky." She turned to the trooper. "Do you need to call for fire and rescue? For the grass fire, I mean?"

He looked up and registered how quickly the flames were multiplying. "Some first responders are on the way, but I'd better report this new problem. Let them know they need a decent-sized pumper out, too."

Briggs made his way around the trailer, still shaking a little from his adrenaline surge. Probably from the unwanted memories, too. "Madison, stay here."

Her attacker was pretty determined to see the job done. He couldn't let down his guard. If he was still shaking a little from his reaction to the explosive, he would just make every effort to ignore it.

Thankfully, he could hear the faint echo of sirens approaching in the distance. Even if it was just the first round of help coming to set things right, a greater number of people with guns and strong protective instincts would discourage Madison's attacker from trying anything else.

After checking up and down the highway again for any signs of the SUV, Briggs walked back around the end of the overturned trailer to Madison, whom he found gently chattering to the still-nervous calves, triggered again by the explosion. They were wide-eyed and shaking. An occasional rebel would spook again, setting them all off once more, but they had settled somewhat.

"Madison, I want you to go sit in the patrol car and close and lock the doors. I'll let the trooper know, but you shouldn't be out here in the open." Briggs directed her toward the black Charger with the Oklahoma State Highway Patrol emblem on the side.

She shrank back. "You want me to just sit in there? Won't you need help when the other trailer arrives?"

"I want you to stay safe and out of the way."

He realized his mistake as soon as she stiffened. "Do you just want me out of sight? Because I doubt he will try again with a whole crew of first responders on the scene. Or do you just think I'll be in the way because there are cattle involved? I was raised on a ranch. Can you say the same?"

Briggs fought a grin. She was fighting mad now. "Yeah, actually. In Wyoming."

"Then you should know that being a woman has no bearing on whether or not a person knows how to help with cattle." She stepped closer to him.

His lip was still twitching. "No, I guess it doesn't. But all I meant was that you've been through a lot already this morning."

She gave an abrupt nod. "Yes, and I'd like to keep my mind off of it."

He considered her for a moment. "I guess I can understand that."

She waited, he could only assume for confirmation that he had changed his mind.

"Just…keep an eye on the road in case the SUV comes back. And if I say go take cover, do it without asking questions." He knew he was wearing a dark scowl—he couldn't help it—but she didn't cower at all.

"Yes, sir." She actually grinned. How was she so unruffled by everything going on? Shouldn't she be shaking in her boots, so to speak?

Briggs shook his head and turned to assess the tasks at hand. He could feel her eyes on him, and he knew she was probably still wondering what had happened back there with the explosive. No doubt she would question him about it later, but he would be ready. No way was he opening up that discussion to someone he had only just met.

He was relieved to see his neighbor returning, trailer in tow, just behind the arrival of initial first responders. Now the real challenge was about to begin.

Once the fire was out, the first responders congregated around the two stock trailers, watching as Seth carefully backed his gooseneck trailer up to the end of Briggs's overturned trailer. As Seth got close, Briggs motioned for him to stop so he could open the back gate of the trailer. He kept the calves enclosed until the chance of escape was minimal, and without direction or question, the first responders filled in the cracks and began helping herd the animals into the upright trailer. Madison, too, was there, coaxing calves from the overturned trailer into the new one. He tried not to notice her, but he couldn't help himself.

"Whoa, hey! Get back in there!" One of the first responders, a neighbor he knew as Caleb, shooed a calf back in the direction he was supposed to be going. Madison laughed, and Briggs was distracted again. She seemed relaxed with all the people around, and when she grinned at Caleb, Briggs found himself envying the guy. Did she know him from when she lived here before?

He shook off his questions and closed the

back gate of Seth's trailer as the last calf hopped in with his herd mates. "That went more smoothly than I anticipated. Thanks, guys."

He shook the hand of the nearest first responder, Rick Donnelly, and proceeded to shake hands with several of the others. Caleb was talking to Madison when he made his way around to him, and Briggs cleared his throat. Flirting was more like it.

Madison tucked a stray hair behind her ear as she turned to Briggs. "Did you know Caleb won the big bull-riding competition in Ada last weekend?"

Briggs shook his head, trying to keep the disapproval from his face. Really? The guy was bragging about winning some bull-riding contest at a time like this? Didn't he know her life was in danger?

"I really think it's best we get you out of here before they come back."

Madison's expression sobered. "Oh. Of course. So the calves are all set? Are we going with Seth?"

"No. He's going to drop them at the stockyards for me. The sheriff is going to take us back to the ranch. A wrecker is headed this way for the truck and trailer, but I feel like it's risky to keep you here any longer."

"When did you talk to the sheriff?"

He tried not to let his irritation show at all of her questions. "While you were watching them put out the fire."

"It was great talking to you, Madison," Caleb said. "Maybe we'll run into each other again."

She smiled at him. "If so, I hope it's under better circumstances."

Caleb nodded and mumbled something in agreement as Briggs gave him a curt nod and put a hand on Madison's arm to lead her away.

As they sat waiting in the back seat of the SUV the sheriff's patrol used, Madison called him out on his behavior. "What was that all about? Are we really in such a hurry?"

Briggs felt ridiculous. He knew he had

no claim on Madison, but he'd wanted to get her away from Caleb. "I just don't want you out in the open in case your attacker decides to try something a little bolder." He turned to look out the window after she nodded. When she didn't respond immediately, he thought she might let the conversation go. He hoped.

She was looking at him intently, though.

"Was there an explosion when Wade died?"

"What did you just say?" Briggs looked frightening, but Madison put on her best investigative reporter face and didn't back down.

"Was there an explosion during the operation where Wade died?" She said it softly, yet with a forceful quality she used to get answers out of interviewees. She felt a little bit bad about hitting him with that kind of shock, but she wanted answers.

"And why would you ask that?" Briggs searched her face, but she had the feeling he was trying to gather his thoughts and buy time.

"Because of your reaction to the explosion, of course. I was just wondering if it had anything to do with the night Wade died." She shifted in the seat, turning her whole upper body to face him.

He responded by turning his face away.

"I really want to know what happened, Briggs." True, she was prodding, but she hoped he would sense her empathy. She just needed answers, partly for her own peace of mind, but also because she found she wanted to understand Briggs better.

"For what? So you can write a story about it? I don't need you exploiting my failures in some big feature article in the next edition of the *newspaper*."

His voice was harsh, angry, and someone without her experience asking the hard questions might shrink back from it.

Madison didn't. "No. I'm asking for personal reasons. I want to know about what happened to Wade. About what happened to you."

"What makes you think I want to let you into my personal life? I don't even know you." Briggs didn't respond well to her prodding. His forehead beaded with sweat, and he closed his eyes, squeezing them shut.

She didn't get to answer, for the door to the patrol vehicle opened and one of the uniformed men hopped in. "Looks like you guys are finally out of here. Back to the ranch?"

The question was directed at Briggs, and he nodded. "I think it's best we get Miss Burke back there right now. Seth is getting the load of calves to the stockyards for me. Madison's father will be concerned."

Was he looking to put off answering her questions? She could learn more once they were safe at the ranch. She felt a little guilty for pushing for answers after how he responded, but she still wanted to know and hoped he would eventually trust her with the whole story. For once, it wasn't mere curiosity. His comment about not wanting to allow her into his personal life stung, even though what he said was true. He didn't know her well enough to trust her, but she was trusting him with her life. Why couldn't he trust her with his past?

The trio rode back to the ranch in near silence after Briggs and the sheriff's deputy exchanged a few remarks about the incident. Her father waited for them on the porch, likely unable to ignore the significance of the patrol vehicle coming up the driveway. Concern emanated from his already wan face and sagging shoulders.

"I'll tell your father what happened if you want to go in and rest." Briggs made the offer near her ear, leaning close so their chauffeur wouldn't hear.

"Thanks, but I'm fine. How about I make some coffee and we tell him about it together?" She was gripping the door handle, but he stopped her.

"Try not to worry, Madison. I think he can handle it." His fingers slid from her forearm.

Briggs's sincere concern touched her. She felt even worse about her treatment of him earlier. "I don't think we can keep it from him. He's bound to hear about it eventually."

He nodded his agreement. "You're probably right. It should come from us."

He popped the door open, and she was surprised when he turned to offer her his assistance from the SUV. He bade the sheriff farewell and thanked him after seeing Madison from the back seat.

Her father waited silently as the sheriff backed up and drove away, and Madison stopped on her way to the front door to hug him. "I'm going to make some coffee. It's a long story, and I know you will want to hear all about it. We might as well have coffee and get comfortable."

Jake's gaze slid toward Briggs, who cued Madison to go on in.

She reached for the doorknob just as a bullet cracked against the door frame beside her head. Her adrenaline immediately skyrocketed, and she dropped low and pushed the door open, ducking into the house as the report of a long-range rifle echoed nearby. A scream welled up within her, but she refused to let it out.

Briggs and Jake had dropped low behind her. Briggs sprang into action, shielding Jake from any additional shots as he drew his Glock and urged Jake into the house. A window near the door shattered with the impact of a new bullet. The shooter wouldn't give up so easily. Madison reached for her father as he came through the door. It didn't escape her notice that he was ashen and trembling.

The adrenaline was having a life-threatening effect on Jake thanks to his heart condition. It took every remaining ounce of calm Madison had to coax him to the floor behind the nearby sofa. She prayed silently all the while, especially that he would remain upright until they got him there.

The shooter continued to pepper the side of the house with bullets, fraying Madison's nerves even further. She wondered about Briggs, but her father's shaking was her biggest concern. He was trying to tell her that he was fine and could make it on his own, but she knew better.

"See about Briggs," he managed to say. He waved toward the door, but the movement was weak.

Madison breathed a momentary breath of relief that he hadn't fallen. "I'll do that, Dad, as soon as I'm convinced you're okay. What do I need to do? Call an ambulance? Get you an aspirin?"

He shook his head. "There's a prescription from my doctor, but it's in the barn loft. I forgot about the medicine when I gathered my things." A gasp cut off his words for a heartbeat. "It'll have to wait."

Madison shook her head. "It can't wait. Dad, you need it. I'm going out the back. Hopefully, no one will notice."

He shook his head. "No! You are young. If it's between your life and mine, you have the most reason to live. You—" His face contorted. "You can't risk it."

She dropped down to one knee beside him. "Dad. I won't sacrifice your life for mine. I'm going. It's a risk I'm just going to have to take. I think I can get to the barn and back before the shooter even knows I'm gone. Pray. Just pray."

She knew she was taking advantage of the fact that he was too weak to stop her at the moment, but she had to save him.

Madison was halfway across the yard before any new shots were fired. She didn't stop to wonder if her attacker had discovered her position or was still firing at the front of the house. The shooter might have figured it out, and she had no intention of giving them more time to reposition for a better shot. Was she even visible to the shooter?

She kept sprinting, even as her question was answered. A bullet struck near her left foot, kicking up a tiny mushroom cloud of dust and debris. She dove for the barn. Thankfully, the big sliding door was open.

When she slid the track door shut with a thundering finality, she leaned against it for only a moment, taking in some much-needed oxygen before heading up the steps to the loft. Once she had retrieved the bottles of medicine next to her father's bed, she made her way back down, still panting with effort.

When she reached the door, she drew a deep breath, preparing to run full speed back to the house. It was hard to hit a moving target, right? Especially if she ran in a zigzag. She slid the door back to make a break for it, but Briggs met her there, glaring and motioning her back inside. He was breathing with effort as well.

"What do you think you are doing?" His face was red with fury.

"It's Dad. He needs his medicine." Madison held out the bottles.

Briggs shook his head in consternation. "Why didn't you tell me? I would have gotten them."

He took the bottles from her hand and stepped toward the house. "Stay here until I come back. The shooter is using a long-range rifle, and I can be back before he can get here."

Madison wanted to protest, but Briggs was gone, the door thudding closed behind him. She hoped he was right about the shooter being a long way off. She drew a deep breath to calm her anxious thoughts. Although she listened intently, she heard no more shots fired. She did, however, hear the sound of sirens. She hoped that meant the sheriff's patrol was about to capture the person who was shooting at her.

It seemed like an eternity before Briggs returned. She made good use of her time by getting to know the horses in his absence. She was leaning against a stall door talking to a big bay gelding whose name plate said "Thor" and stroking his nose when Briggs came back in.

"My horse doesn't like many people." His voice startled her.

She turned to face him. "Thor?" She indicated the name plate on his stall door.

He grinned. "I like Marvel movies." The shrug he added made him look boyish.

"Is Dad okay?" She tried to dismiss the effect his action had.

"He's fine. Resting. And the shooter is gone. The sheriff's patrol officer chased him off the property. He managed to sneak away through the trees along the road, but they are going to keep looking for him." Briggs stepped closer.

Thor pulled away, tossing his head. Madison spoke softly to the gelding, and he arched his neck back over the side of the stall and laid his forehead against her head.

Briggs shook his head. "Unbelievable. I turn my back, and the big goober betrays me."

Madison laughed softly. "We were just talking. He probably sensed I needed some comfort. Horses are experts at reading emotions."

Briggs rolled his eyes as she gave Thor's blaze a thorough rub, sending the tiny white hairs scattering over his head.

"Or he likes that you're spoiling him. Did you give him a treat, also?" Briggs looked like he was trying to frown, but she thought his lips were twitching.

"Only one. Or two. I can't remember for sure." Her own lips twitched.

"Oh, mercy." Briggs sighed. "Like father,

like daughter, I guess. Your dad loves to spoil the animals, too. He thinks no one knows."

Madison stepped away from the stall. "Then we will keep his secret. Can I go back to the house now? I'm worried about him."

"Of course. Let's go." Briggs extended a hand, and they hurried back to the house to check on her father.

Madison moved to her father's side, relieved to find him resting peacefully, as Briggs had said. She offered him a smile and squeezed his hand. "See, Dad? I'm back, safe and sound."

Jake's gaze cut toward Briggs, but he didn't say anything.

"I'm sure you tried to stop her, but she was right that you needed your meds. You wouldn't have held up much longer without them." Briggs stepped closer to them both, his broad shoulders taking up a good deal of space in the room.

Madison nodded. "So I'm not as foolish as you let on."

Briggs frowned. "I didn't say it wasn't foolish for you to take that risk."

She must have looked shocked. "But— I mean, you just said..."

"I said he needed them. I didn't say it was a good idea for you to go get them." He reached into a large basket at the foot of the sofa and pulled out a blanket. He handed it to Madison.

She paused to study him a moment before spreading the blanket over her father, who accepted it gratefully. "What would you have had me do?"

"You should have let me get it." He turned to go into the kitchen.

She followed him. "And how should I have done that? Stick my head out the front door amid the gunfire to let you know he needed it?"

Behind her, Jake made a noise she thought might have been a muffled laugh. He coughed weakly and waved off her searching look when she turned.

Briggs didn't stop walking, just shrugged

one shoulder as he went. "Better than running out into the open."

Madison stopped, throwing up her hands. "There were no shots being fired out back."

He spun to face her now. "Not until you ran across the backyard. I'm trying to keep you from being killed here."

She avoided his eyes. "I know. But I couldn't just stand by and watch him suffer and grow sicker."

His demeanor softened then. "I understand. I just need to ask you to think before you do things like that."

She sighed. "I didn't see any other option."

He nodded then. "Truce over coffee? I have some decaf for your dad if he wants some."

The deputy knocked on the door then, and Briggs invited him in and offered him coffee as well. The deputy accepted and waited with her father.

To her surprise, Briggs accompanied her to the kitchen, and not only helped make coffee, but also retrieved some brownies from the back of a counter nearby, cutting them neatly and sliding them onto small plates.

"The deputy will stick around as a deterrent, in case any other attempts are made on your life." His tone had turned matter-of-fact, the rich emotion that had filled his voice only a moment ago gone.

"That's reassuring." She set four heavy mugs on the counter beside the gurgling coffee maker.

"I did some intelligence work while I was in the SEALs. If you can help me with some information, it's likely we can figure this whole thing out." He was adding forks to the plates where the large squares of chocolaty brownies waited.

Madison felt her stomach flip. She was less than thrilled at the idea of anyone digging into her past. "Information like what?"

The rich scent of chocolate mingled enticingly with the brewing coffee as Briggs added the final fork to the brownie plates.

"Well, start wherever you are most comfortable, but I suspect the answer lies in your not-so-distant past. Controversial stories you have written? Failed relationships? Friendships gone bad? School or career competition?"

"Is this your way of finding out the dirt on me?" Madison teased, but he frowned, so she sobered also.

"I really want to help, but you aren't taking this seriously." His jaw set like a pillar of stone.

Madison thought for a moment. "I've experienced my share of all of that, but none really to the extent that would drive someone to want to kill me."

"You don't know that. Maybe it's something beneath the surface. Well-hidden. How about we start with the articles?" Briggs glanced at the near-finished coffeepot.

"Well, I write a lot of articles on educational reform. Not really something that would make me a target for a killer." She shrugged. "Recently I've picked up some stories on politics, the human trafficking problems, and drug law reform. I guess any of those issues could spark some anger."

Briggs was looking off into the air. "That's true, but that doesn't really narrow it down. Can I get copies of your stories from the last six months to a year? Maybe we can build a list of suspects and narrow it down from there."

Madison nodded and leaned in to pick up some of the plates while Briggs poured the freshly brewed coffee, but her buzzing phone stopped her. She looked at the screen to see the contact name.

"It's my friend Adria calling from Boston. She promised to call when she knew something. I'd better talk to her. I'll be right there." She left Briggs standing in the kitchen to move to the bedroom down the hall.

"Hi, Adie, what's up?" Madison knew why her friend was calling, but she forced a light tone.

"Madi, are you okay? Oh, please tell me

you're all right!" Adria's voice was near panicked.

"I guess you heard there was another attack." Madison wandered into her room, closed the door softly, and sat down on the bed.

"Of course I heard. The Oklahoma police won't let Davis off the phone for more than three minutes at a time. He's about to combust." Adria's voice didn't calm much.

"They've been pretty diligent about the investigation, huh?" Madison was a little shaken by the seriousness of the situation.

"Yes, apparently shooting up the Oklahoma City airport gets taken pretty seriously in light of the town's history." Adria was referring to the bombing of a large federal building in the city back in the midnineties. "And now they are running you off the road and tossing explosives at you. Who would do such crazy things?"

"I don't know." Madison gripped the phone a little more tightly. "Briggs, the guy I told you about last night, suspects it could be someone we work with, since the attacks started before I left Boston. Do you think he could be right?"

Adria drew in a sharp breath. "Surely not! Who could it be? We work with a pretty boring, laid-back group of people. That just seems too far-fetched. It couldn't be someone you know, could it?"

Madison hesitated. "It's just that I seem to be a target. I don't know who I could have offended so badly or why. And whoever is doing this seems to know me well. I haven't written about anyone I know."

"Could it be that they've just really done their homework?" Adria quieted. When Madison didn't answer, she continued. "Either way, I was calling to let you know I'm on my way. You need your best friend there for support."

"You're coming here?" Madison was surprised. "I don't think that's a good idea. It's too risky."

"I'll be okay. I can take care of myself, Madi. Besides, I can't wait to see this hunky former SEAL you've got protecting you." Adria giggled.

Madison wasn't convinced. "Ah. You've googled Briggs Thorpe. Speaking of doing your homework..." She trailed off.

"Yes, I always do. Occupational habits, I guess." Adria was still sounding like it wasn't a big deal.

Madison took a deep breath. "Really, though, Adria. I don't think you should come to Oklahoma right now. It isn't safe, and we have all we can handle going on right now. Wouldn't you rather come some-time when I can really show you around and we can enjoy ourselves?"

Adria blew off her concerns. "I fully intend to help protect you. That's what friends do. It will help to have someone else watching out for you. And I'm not coming to vacation. I just want to help look out for my best friend. I need to see for myself that you're okay."

Madison didn't know what else to say. Her instincts told her it wasn't a good idea, but she was out of arguments. She prayed that Adria wouldn't become col-lateral damage, but she knew her friend was strong-willed and wouldn't be easily persuaded. She would have to keep trying, though. If Adria came to Oklahoma, she might be endangering her own life. Madison reminded her of that fact before ending the call. She stared at the phone in thought for a long moment after disconnecting.

Madison's attention was diverted from her concerns, however, when she heard a scratching at the window. Telling herself she was probably just being paranoid, she glanced in that direction. She didn't see anything, so she moved closer to the window. A shadow from the overhang of the eaves distorted her view, but a tree limb stuck out close by. She sighed. Surely that was the source of the noise she had heard.

She turned and was about to open the door to leave when there was a sharp cracking noise. Knowing beyond a doubt that a tree limb couldn't have made such a loud noise, she hit the floor, a scream escaping as she tumbled down.

Another sharp crack echoed through the room as if someone were trying to break the window. Madison screamed again, trying to reach the doorknob to pry it open, but the sound of glass shattering caused her to shrink back.

A rock tumbled through, thudding to a stop near her feet just as a black leather-gloved hand reached through the broken pane.

FIVE

The door wrenched open, and Madison shrieked again, startled by the movement. Briggs rushed past her as the black-clad hand slipped back through the broken pane. The shadow of a man's form dressed in camouflage material dashed past the window.

Briggs crossed the room and held his Glock out the window to try to get off a shot at the fleeing figure. For a second, his hand hovered there, waiting to get the perp in his sights. It was too dark and he lost visual.

"Ahh!" He groaned aloud as he pulled it back through the broken glass. "Are you okay?"

When he looked her way again, Madison reassured him. "Yes. I'm fine."

"The deputy left while you were on the phone. Went to make a pass around the property. I'm going to go after the shooter. Stay here." He took off.

Once he was gone, she tried to see Briggs moving across the tree-speckled yard through the shards of the window glass. An occasional shadow shifted but that was all she could make out.

The two figures had disappeared from view. She heard Briggs shouting at the man to stop, and soon a shot followed. She prayed it was from Briggs's Glock and not a weapon held by the man he pursued.

She called 911 and reported the series of events. After she disconnected, there was still nothing to see outside her window.

The seconds seemed to inch by as she waited for Briggs to reappear. Her anxiety grew, and she was about to give up and go out looking for him when he appeared once more in the yard. He was shaking his head, and a grim expression covered his face. Obviously, the perp had gotten away.

A patrol car barreled up the driveway, and she looked toward the sound of crackling gravel. Briggs ducked over to speak to the officer behind the wheel, and Madison slipped out of the bedroom to meet him outside.

"I winged him, but he still somehow managed to get away. That was my fault for not shooting a little closer to the middle of him," Briggs told the officer with an animated expression. "I just wanted to slow him down."

The officer agreed he had done the right thing. "Err on the side of caution. He'll show up in a nearby ER soon enough."

"Do you really think you can track him down?" Madison asked him after she told her part of the story. She knew fear bled through in her voice, but it had been too close a call to get over easily. The sight of someone breaking into her window was just a little too much.

"There's a good chance. Sounds like he'll

need treatment for a gunshot wound. Not many hunting accidents this time of year, either, so it'll be hard to hide." The officer pressed his lips together.

"If he goes for treatment… There's a chance he might not." Briggs gave her a sympathetic look. Was he trying to keep her from getting her hopes too high?

"Either way, we'll catch him soon, ma'am. We are doing everything we can." The officer gave her a reassuring smile and drove away.

Madison followed Briggs back into the house but went to the kitchen for a drink of water. She needed a moment to catch her breath. She knew her father was still waiting to talk to her, too.

Briggs thought Madison's color had returned somewhat by the time she joined the men in the living room. Her countenance had relaxed some as well. Maybe hearing from her friend had done her some good.

The officer they had spoken to outside

had promised to update the deputy patrolling around the property. He'd also said they would increase the patrol in light of this new development.

After filling her father in on the recent danger, Madison told them about her phone call with her friend.

"Adria is insisting on coming here," Madison announced. "I have tried to discourage her. I told her it's too dangerous right now, but she says she isn't that easily deterred. Is there a good hotel I could recommend somewhere not too far from the ranch? It's been a long time since I've lived here."

"No, that much hasn't changed. I can't say there are any decent hotels within miles of here." Briggs wore a scowl. "But you're right. She really should stay away for the time being."

Madison agreed. "I would love to talk her out of it. Do you have any ideas?"

Briggs shook his head. "Unfortunately, I don't know what else to tell her, either. At least invite her to stay here if she won't keep her distance. There's plenty of room here, and that way we can be sure she is safe also." Briggs gestured vaguely around the spacious house.

Madison's countenance brightened a bit. "Honestly, that would be great. Are you sure you don't mind?"

"Of course not. I'm sure having another female here will be a comfort to you, considering you don't know Mrs. Newman all that well." Briggs lifted his coffee mug and gestured for her to sit down.

She settled in with them, and they began to discuss the events from earlier in the day up to the most recent invasion. Briggs promised to get her window repaired quickly and explained he would soon be taking his truck for repairs as well.

"Honestly, I might have to replace the truck and trailer both after all of this, but I'll worry about that when the time comes," Briggs said as his phone went off.

He answered it and spoke only a few words before moving out to the porch.

When he came back in, he looked at Madison first. "Good news and bad. The guy showed up at a local small-town ER. He's just a hired guy. He doesn't know anything, was just looking to make some drug money."

Briggs watched Madison's reaction go from hopeful to disappointed again. He couldn't help but wonder how she was holding up. The last twenty-four hours had been very eventful for her, and he knew the shock would catch up to her soon. After a few moments, he noticed her eyes were getting heavy, and her attention was drifting.

"Is there anything else?" she asked Briggs.

He shook his head. "No, I think that's about it." Which was good, because she didn't look like she could tolerate much more right now.

He wouldn't forget her frightened reaction to the day's events. Her wide eyes and quaking limbs had belied her bravado. He admired the fact that she hadn't let the fear overcome her, however. Other than the moment earlier today when he had prodded her to call 911 before the trailer incident, she hadn't let the fear affect her. He had witnessed plenty of soldiers in battle who couldn't say the same.

He hoped she would be able to rest tonight. He knew how difficult it could be to sleep after such traumatic events. He still had trouble sleeping most nights, thanks to his years in the navy.

Today had brought back far too many unpleasant memories for him, memories he had suppressed for a long time. Was God trying to tell him it was time to deal with them?

After the explosion that had taken Wade's life, he had been honorably discharged from duty due to physical restrictions. He had temporarily lost partial vision in his left eye in the explosion. They had been unsure at the time if it would fully return or not. It had taken some time. Mentally, he had been relieved, though. He hadn't been certain he could pass the psych evaluation, anyway.

At that point, he had come to Oklahoma to try to make things right with Wade's parents, hoping it might provide a balm for his grief. Wade had come along late in his parents' lives, and he had often spoken of the numerous problems they faced with health and finances. The Whitsons had been forgiving, assuring him they didn't blame him, but it hadn't been enough for Briggs.

Before Briggs left, Wade's father fell seriously ill, and with nothing else pressing to do, Briggs had offered to stay and help. During that time, Wade's mother had asked him to take her to church, since she had been advised not to drive because of her own declining health. He had complied, finding he was glad to get back into the routine of attending as he had as a youth. Soon, he found God to be the comfort that saw him through that tough time in his life. He learned to pray and lean on God when the trauma and guilt became overwhelming. He wasn't completely free from it, but he was getting better one day at a time.

He wondered if Madison was a believer. She had lived away from here for a long time, and he didn't know a lot about her current life in the city. He knew her dad was a Christian, and she had a certain goodness about her that spoke of a strong faith, but he didn't want to ask.

"Tomorrow is Sunday. We usually go to the early church service in town, but maybe we should watch the service online instead. Do you want to join us?"

When Madison smiled, it gave him the answer he hoped for. "Of course. Should I just come to the living room?"

The men both nodded. Her father began to tell her about the church they attended, and she said it sounded great. Things had grown quiet around the ranch, but the atmosphere was still charged. He knew better than to think Madison's attacker had given up. Briggs had things to get done, but he would just have to bring Madison along. She likely wouldn't mind, and he had better take advantage of the stillness while it lasted.

Because he was certain it wouldn't last.

Madison had spent the day following Briggs around and trying to stay out of his way. He made her feel safe even when his attention seemed to be focused elsewhere, and she liked it. He didn't say a whole lot as he went about his ranch work, but she enjoyed the fresh air and the contentment that accompanied her as they rode across the fields in his UTV. She hadn't realized how much she had missed home.

Home.

Was that how she felt about this place? She hadn't thought she would ever return here to live. Before now, she had believed herself to be happy in the city. She had friends there, and she did enjoy her job, but this trip was making her question that decision.

She knew she had to figure out a plan for when Adria arrived. "I need to ask you about something. It's Adria. I can't talk her out of coming."

Briggs looked at her from his place in the driver's seat of the UTV, and she explained further. "She texted me again earlier. Her plane will be here at four."

"That's in a couple of hours. We'll have to finish up some things after we pick her up." Briggs put both hands on the wheel of the UTV, still seeming lost in thought. She assumed he was trying to figure out a plan for her friend's arrival.

His truck had been taken for repairs, but the ranch had a midsize Ford SUV he kept around for convenience. It had been his only transportation before buying the truck. She knew she was interfering with his work to go and pick up her friend at the airport and felt bad about it.

"Is that going to be an inconvenience for you? I could pick her up and just take Dad along." Madison was feeling more secure now that things seemed to have quieted down. The local sheriff had stationed a patrol car on the ranch as well as an officer who patrolled the perimeter of the property every half hour.

She could see from Briggs's expression that he was never going to agree to that idea. "It isn't an inconvenience at all, but she might want to have her own transportation. Are you sure she can't be discouraged from coming?"

When Madison gave an exasperated sigh, he continued. "Well, then I guess you could suggest she rent a car, if that wouldn't be too much trouble for her. You have your dad's truck if you need it, and frankly, I don't want you going anywhere alone, anyway, but she might need a car, depending on how long she's staying and what her plans are while she's here."

They had been repairing some barbed wire fencing on the west side of the property while the hands rounded up some rogue heifers that had broken through it, and he began to load all the wire, clips, and other tools back into the UTV.

"I'll send her a text to see if she wants to rent a car. If so, I can drop her a pin once her plane lands, and we can meet her at the house when she arrives. That way we won't interrupt any work you need to get done." Madison smiled.

He had a light shadow of whiskers taking over the lower half of his chiseled face, and she tried not to notice how good he looked with his hat pulled low over his blue eyes. He stopped loading the fencing supplies into the UTV. "So do we need to leave, or finish the fence repairs first?"

He gestured to the next stretch of loose wire down the fence line.

"I think we have time." She didn't want to keep him from getting his work done. Those heifers had to stay separated from the bulls until they were old enough to safely breed. Young heifers bred too early usually resulted in the loss of life of either the cow, calf, or both.

"Okay. Let me know as soon as you hear something." Briggs pulled the UTV to the next area of fence that needed patching. Madison got out and helped him as much as she could by handing him tools, holding wire in place, and occasionally bending a clip or two around a T-post. She pulled out her phone and checked for a reply every so often.

Briggs caught her once and chuckled. "It's okay. We will figure it out."

The sound of his deep chuckle made her insides swirl just a bit, and Madison redirected her attention to the task at hand, ashamed of her lack of focus.

She stood close to Briggs beside the fence, tapping her foot impatiently as she waited for a reply. They loaded back up to move to the next area of fence that needed repair. He took a T-post from her hands with a wink and asked her to bring him the nearly empty spool of wire. She handled it carefully to avoid sticking herself on the sharp new barbs.

She was about to give up on hearing back from Adria in time and suggest they go on to the airport when her friend replied at last.

"She decided a rental is a good idea. I'll go ahead and drop her a pin now." Madison let out a relieved breath. "I really wish she would have just stayed in Boston."

"I wish she would have, too. What about your pets? Is she the one taking care of them?"

"She's bringing them with her." Madison shrugged.

They drove to the front of the house to retrieve a flathead shovel he had left near the flower beds.

"A cottonmouth got a little too close to the house yesterday." His explanation made perfect sense to Madison, but she could imagine trying to explain to Adria how a shovel made an ideal weapon for beheading a poisonous snake. Adria had grown up in New York City. She probably wouldn't relate to poisonous snakes too well.

A splintered place in the wood of the porch drew her attention away from the shovel, reminding her there was more danger to be concerned with than just a venomous snake. Someone was determined to kill her. The bullet holes marred several other places on Briggs's porch.

"Your beautiful porch is destroyed." It was an exaggeration, but she hated to see the ugly reminders of the shooter's determination.

"Those holes are an easy fix. As long as none of them hit you, repairing a bit of splintered wood is irrelevant to me. There is always something that needs fixing on a ranch." He sent a crooked grin her way, and she swallowed hard.

The attraction she felt for Briggs was just compounding her mental confusion. She was having trouble keeping her thoughts from dwelling on him. Even though she knew Adria would be safer in Boston, she was a little relieved she would soon be here to help Madison keep from spending so much alone time with Briggs.

Too much time with Briggs could be dangerous to her heart.

Briggs watched the two women greet each other on the front porch. His gut clenched as he wondered if he would have two women to try to protect now instead of one. Adria seemed oblivious to the additional trouble she might be causing, making him wonder what sort of person she was. He knew it wasn't fair to feel that way. He didn't know her at all, and maybe she was just deeply concerned about Madison and genuinely thought she could help.

The two ladies exchanged a hug and began to chatter like teenagers while Madison pulled her calico cat from the carrier and held him. Briggs shook his head, hoping to dismiss his misgivings, and moved away to give them some space.

As he left, he overheard Adria telling Madison that her Pomeranian had put up quite a fuss on the plane. Madison was promising to reimburse Adria for traveling fees for the animals, and the tiny canine squeaked in excitement as Madison freed it as well.

Briggs shut the front door behind him, and Jake pointed to the chair near the sofa. "Might as well hang with me for a while.

Those two will be catching up for a bit, no doubt."

"Yeah, probably. I'll get us a drink."

Briggs brought Jake a glass of sweet iced tea from the kitchen and settled in to give him the report on the ranch operations. "I still have heifers to check, but I will give Madison and her friend some time to chat before I drag Madison away again. I assume Adria will wanna stay here at the house while we work."

Jake gave a chuckle. "From what I've seen of her so far, she doesn't look much like she's dressed to go traipsing through a cow pasture. She can stay here with me and rest up from her flight."

"I think that's a good idea." Briggs nodded. "It's been quiet since the patrol car arrived."

Jake pressed his lips together. "Yep, maybe too quiet. I know you're probably itchin' to catch the shooter. I know I would be if I was able."

Briggs frowned back at him. "You have no idea how much. I just hope she doesn't let her guard down too much now that her friend is here. I don't want her to be stressed, but not being careful enough could get them both killed. I don't know what her friend was thinking coming here, but it's only going to complicate things."

Jake looked out the window to where the women still stood talking. Briggs had taken Adria's luggage to her room and told them to catch up. They were still talking away, but Madison glanced around her every so often, as if making sure it was still safe.

The sheriff's patrol car sat a few yards away. Briggs knew the other deputy had just made a pass around the perimeter of the ranch, and another deputy was due to relieve the one by the house in about a half hour. The sheriff's office was good to check in with him every so often, and the last report had turned up very little. There had been a few shell casings found, but either they were left over from hunters last fall, or the casings had been left to try and throw them off the shooter's trail, because the ballistics didn't match the long-range rifle from the airport shooting. Of course, there was always the possibility that they were using more than one type of gun.

"Still haven't heard any more from your brother, I guess?" Jake pulled Briggs's attention back to the present moment.

"No, Avery said he would call by tonight with a report. I'd like to do a little digging myself, but I haven't had a chance so far. As soon as Madison goes to bed tonight, I plan to do some of my own research." Briggs took a long drink of water. He needed to get the facts straight in his head.

"I have no doubt you will figure it out soon." Jake set his own water glass on a coaster atop the nearby side table.

The women came in at that moment, and Madison made the introductions between Adria and her father.

"Pardon me for not getting up," Jake began.

"Oh, no. Please don't get up on my account. Madi told me you've had a bit of trouble with your health lately. It's a pleasure to meet you." Adria reached a dainty hand toward him, her smile charming. She was petite and well-dressed, her silk button-down blouse accented with a graceful set of pearls that circled a slender neck. Her blue eyes were so pale they were almost colorless, and her hair was dark and sleek. It was swept up on top of her head except for a few wisps hanging carefully around her face.

Jake seemed enchanted. "It's my pleasure, miss. Madison speaks well of you."

"Oh, thank you. I'll be sure to watch out for her." Adria laughed and squeezed his hand. She turned and looked at Madison, who rolled her eyes.

"What are you gonna do, Adie? You aren't any bigger than a seed tick." Madison teased.

"Oh, listen to that. One day back in the country... It didn't take long at all." Adria waved a hand.

"You know I always snuck in a few countryisms, even in Boston." Madison laughed. "You know what they say about taking the girl out of the country."

Briggs cut in then amid their giggling. "I put Adria's luggage in the first bedroom on the right. It's the closest to yours, Madison."

The two women looked at him and smiled.

"Perfect. Adie, I'll show you where it is if you want to change or rest." Madison led Adria to the room Briggs had mentioned.

She returned in a few seconds without her friend. "Adria is going to rest for a bit. Sounds like she had a tough flight."

"I am, too, if y'all don't mind." Jake yawned from the couch. "Go on and take care of the rest of the chores. I fully intend to be back on my feet doing the lion's share of the work tomorrow."

Madison shook her head. "We'll see about that when tomorrow comes."

Briggs approached a bit hesitantly when he caught Madison alone in the living room a little later that day.

"I know you've had a trying day, but we really need to go check cows. I have several first-calf heifers due to calve any day." Briggs turned Madison's attention away from her father's health for the moment. There would be plenty of time to argue with Jake about how much work he could do later.

She felt a little thrill of excitement. When she was a girl, she had loved calving season. The little newborns with their silky, shiny coats, jumping and playing on their wobbly little legs, were so adorable. "Okay, I'll change into some jeans. I don't have boots anymore, but I brought an old pair of running shoes."

Briggs nodded. "Mrs. Whitson might have some you could wear if you'd rather."

She rose to go down the hall. "I can check."

"Do you think you can still ride okay? I know you said you thought so, but are you comfortable with it?" he asked.

She grinned. "A horse? Of course I can."

"She grew up on a horse. I used to think

her backside would end up the shape of that saddle with as much time as she spent riding that gelding of hers." Jake chuckled.

"Nothing like the love between a girl and her horse." Madison sighed, memories of galloping through grassy fields on Scamper's back flitting through her mind as she slipped down the hall. She had named her horse after the legendary gelding ridden by her childhood hero, barrel racer Charmayne James.

Nostalgia filled her as she pulled out a pair of jeans. She had found a pair of boots in Mrs. Whitson's closet that fit her almost perfectly. Wade's mom had a generous nature, and Madison knew she would love to see her boots getting some use. Madison had often ridden out with Wade to check the cows or round up strays and returned to find Mrs. Whitson had made cookies and laid them out with tall glasses of milk. She had watched for them from the window and always known just how long the two kids would goof off in the barn before coming in.

Wade's infectious laughter filled her memory. He'd dared her to do silly things only a country kid would do or threatened to shove her into a pond just to hear her squeal. Once he had talked her into tasting the sweet feed they fed to the show calves. Of course, he had tried it first. Then there was the reason he'd given her the nickname Chop. She had wanted to learn karate, but every time she made a move, she would unexpectedly yell out the word *chop*. Wade had found it hilarious.

She pushed the memories aside as the sadness began to well up in her. They had grown apart in high school, and she hadn't talked to him much after he joined the navy. Losing someone without the chance to say goodbye was always hard, but especially someone so young.

Obviously, Briggs had been greatly affected by his death as well. She hoped he would eventually tell her how close he and Wade had been and what happened.

She returned to find him waiting for her

by the door. "Your father is mad because he has to stay here and rest."

Madison chuckled. She could well imagine her father's current mental state. "He'll get over it. He doesn't need to be up and about."

Briggs murmured his agreement and led the way to the barn. Once there, he pointed her in the direction of a gorgeous buckskin mare. "I think you and KitKat will get along well. Kat for short."

Madison stroked the golden muzzle of the stout little mare he had pointed out. "Oh, she's beautiful."

The mare tossed her head as if acknowledging the compliment, sending the long strands of her silky, blue-black mane dancing.

"It helps that she gets along well with Thor, also." He handed her a bright pink halter.

Madison raised an eyebrow at the color choice. "Pink, huh?"

He laughed at her teasing, but then he grew serious. "She belongs to Mrs. Whitson. She chose the tack for Kat before she became sick."

Madison sobered. "Oh. I'm sorry. I didn't consider that."

He shook his head. "Don't worry about it."

"I'd like to see her if I can. Mrs. Whitson, I mean." Madison had known Mrs. Whitson since she was small. Aside from the cookies, Mrs. Whitson had also made the best homemade chocolate cake that Madison had ever eaten. She was beginning to realize just how much she missed living in a small town, where she knew everyone.

"Sure. I usually go see her on Sunday afternoons and tell her about the church service. When she first started asking me about it, I thought she was just keeping me accountable, and then I realized she just really missed attending in person, even though she still watches the service. I think she is just lonely." He slipped a dark green halter over Thor's nose. "I make a point to go every Sunday for her, even if things are busy on the ranch."

Madison's heart melted like a popsicle on a sunny sidewalk. "That's so thoughtful of you."

He froze with his back toward her. "It's the least I can do."

It was a minute before he moved again, and she wondered what she had said wrong.

"Of course," Madison mumbled, not expecting a response considering his cool manner. They led the horses into the barn aisle and began to groom them and tack them up.

"It was my fault Wade died," Briggs said as he stroked Thor's nose with a small face brush. "I should have been in his place."

When he didn't say anything else, Madison asked, "Why do you think that?"

He dropped the brush and picked up a woolen saddle pad. "I was platoon leader that night. I should have been out front. Wade got ahead of me because I stopped to reprimand one of the other men. Wade just kept going, doing his thing. I turned around to warn him to stop just in time to—"

When Briggs broke off and turned away, she let him, fearful that she knew where the story was going. She simply waited, her chest aching for Briggs...for Wade. For all of them.

"The explosion was merciful enough to kill him instantly, but the image of him being overtaken by flames is never gonna leave me." Briggs didn't turn to face her, and she knew he probably feared all that she might see in his eyes.

"You saw him die." The soft words slipped out, and he surprised her by finally turning toward her.

"Yeah. I had just called out his name, and he turned as it exploded. The look on his face haunts me. It will haunt me for the rest of my life." He drew in a deep breath. "It should have been me. He was an only child. His parents needed him. I have four brothers, and my family is already broken."

Madison smiled sadly. "That doesn't

make you expendable. God always has a greater purpose, even when we don't understand. It can't be laid on your shoulders. And besides, I'm sure your family isn't as broken as you think."

His expression was lost in the past.

"We were best friends. He knew that. Took advantage. I should have been tougher on him. It might have saved his life." Briggs shook his head, hands fisted tightly at his sides now. Anger, at himself, she assumed, radiated from his taut expression. For a moment, she glimpsed the hard-eyed, steel-jawed SEAL he must have been back then.

"I doubt you were easy on him. SEAL life wouldn't allow that. Besides, knowing Wade, I think he would have rather saved your life. He always wanted to be a hero."

"Well, he did. He's definitely a hero. Probably saved our whole unit with his reckless behavior. If he hadn't gotten ahead of us, the explosion probably would have killed us all." Briggs reached for his heavy leather saddle and threw it up onto Thor's back. He began fastening the girth and the thin leather straps that made up the breast collar that went across the gelding's chest, to help hold the saddle securely in place.

Madison realized he didn't intend to say anything more. "I'm glad you told me."

The only acknowledgment that he had heard her was a nod. Madison checked the length of the stirrups as she pondered what had just transpired. Surely she was over-reacting to think it was significant that he had shared this with her. There had to be another justification for his actions other than the one she was considering, the one spreading warmth throughout her.

You know better than to have any warm, fuzzy feelings for any man, she reminded herself. Her former fiancé, Jonas Spencer, had given her every reason to shy away from emotional connections. He had made her believe in true love and fairy tales, only to break her heart, proving he was nothing but a fantastic actor, and she a gull-ible fool.

She would never risk her heart like that again.

She struggled for a moment with the thought of how Jonas had led her to believe she was the love of his life, making promises of rings and white dresses. When he had suddenly told her he didn't want to see her anymore, she was shocked. That shock, however, didn't compare to the shock she felt when he had soon announced an engagement to another woman, his high school sweetheart. Though he had often spoken about her, Jonas had always insisted they were only friends and he no longer had feelings for her. Knowing he had broken off their relationship for his old girlfriend still stung. She had been about to give up her career and move with him before he broke it off. She had been surprised the newspaper had let her stay.

Madison and Briggs finished tacking up the horses and rode out in silence. Somehow, it wasn't awkward. It was a thoughtful silence that closed them off from the rest of the world, and Madison took advantage of the opportunity to contemplate their conversation, replaying Briggs's words over and over again in her mind.

He needed time to heal.

The realization came to her, and she uttered a quick prayer that God would lead him in doing so.

Their ride was uneventful. All the heifers still showed only a mild possibility of calving soon. The buffalo were less of a concern, usually calving easily without help, but they observed them from a distance to rule out any signs of distress among the expectant mothers before riding back to the barn.

They had untacked the horses and were feeding and watering their mounts as well as the three other horses in the barn when Madison heard little rustling noises coming from the far end of the barn. She stood perfectly still for a moment, listening. The hairs on the back of her neck prickled. When Briggs caught sight of her, he raised one eyebrow, but before he could question her, she laid a finger against her lips and pointed.

It was only a moment before he realized she had heard something, and he sprang into action. He was gone before she knew what was happening.

She dropped the feed bucket she held in one hand and followed him. The feed room door to her left swung shut, though, and she halted, turning toward the room. She pushed the door open and looked around inside, finding nothing. Nothing except another door that led outside. She strode over to it, checked the lock, found it unsecured and turned the knob. It stuck for a moment, but with a hard shove, it finally wedged open.

A figure disappeared around the end of the barn just as she put a shoulder against the door and forced it open wide. A loaded wheelbarrow on the other side tumbled over. Someone had tried to slow down her pursuit. She followed the figure around the corner but saw no one in the shadowy overhang from the structure.

"Briggs!" she called out as she hurried back into the barn. She scurried through the feed room and back into the aisle.

"Briggs! Outside. Someone disappeared around the north corner." But there was no answer, so she moved down past the stalls.

There was nothing at this end of the barn but stacked square bales of hay, fifty or sixty pounds apiece, nearly touching the barn's high rafters. She was about to return to the far end of the barn when she heard the rustling again.

"Briggs?" No answer came.

Where had he gone?

The eeriness of the quiet barn, broken only by the horses nosing around in their feed buckets, enveloped her. She contemplated her next move for a long moment. When no other sound came, she grew curious. She approached the corner where the noise had originated from.

At last, the ladder to her father's living quarters creaked. Madison turned with a gasp, only to see Briggs coming down. His long, denim-clad legs came into view just before the rest of him began to materialize.

"Briggs, I'm glad to see you. I didn't know where you—"

"Watch out!" Briggs cut off her words with a shouted warning as he leaped off the ladder toward her.

But it was too late.

She looked up to see an avalanche of square hay bales rushing right toward her head.

SIX

Briggs saw the bales of hay toppling toward Madison from too far away. He rushed at her but couldn't reach her in time to push her from their path or shield her. Flames ignited amid the bales. The whooshing sound he had heard hadn't been his breath leaving his body. Someone had set an explosive to trigger the hay to fall.

Madison froze in place until the last second, probably uncertain of which way to move. Then she tried to stumble out of the way, but one heavy bale caught her on the left side, knocking her to the ground. Another bale bounced onto her, crushing her into the dirt floor. The flames leaped and surged to life, sending the horses into a frenzy.

Briggs felt his stomach lurch, but there was no time to lament the barn fire. He lunged across the barn to get to Madison. The bales were still tumbling and settling all around her, and he had to push some out of the way to get to her side. The heavy dust and chaff thickened the air, and he shielded his nose and mouth, squinting to protect his eyes amid the settling debris. The smoke wafted in right behind it as the dry bales crackled.

Madison was silent, unmoving. Fear clutched at him. He spoke her name, but she didn't stir. He couldn't see her eyes, for she lay on her side facing away from him.

He picked up one of the bales to toss it out of the way and finally heard her whimper. Chucking the bale, he picked up another. When he finally reached her, he knelt beside her.

"Madison, can you hear me? We have to get out of here."

She muttered an affirmative, "I'm fine."

Heat filled the barn. Flames were roaring around them now. One of the hands came running in.

"Everybody okay?" he asked.

"I think so, Stockton. I just need to get her out of here. Can you see to the horses?" Briggs responded loudly to be heard over the sound of the fire raging through the hay. Smoke was filling the barn rapidly now as well.

He looked Madison over only a second more. "I'm going to pick you up. Are you sure your back or neck isn't injured? I don't want to make anything worse."

"I'm sure." Her face scrunched as he picked her up, but she didn't complain. They ducked out of the flaming barn, and as they did, a couple of other hands rushed in to help Stockton with the horses.

"We called the fire department," another hand yelled as he ran in after the horses. The men didn't even pause. Livestock were a huge asset on a ranch and everyone who worked there was willing to risk life and limb to save them.

Briggs thanked him and looked at the

barn anxiously, but he stayed with Madison. He spoke to her gently, and she opened her eyes, slowly blinked and tried to focus on him.

"My shoulder." She winced.

Briggs stopped her. "Let me take a look."

A lot could happen when a huge pile of hay bales fell on a person. She seemed to be mobile everywhere, ruling out any spinal injuries. He wasn't convinced nothing was broken, though.

"Okay. Only my shoulder hurts, though." Madison looked a little frightened.

"Is there any pain in any of your limbs or your head?"

She paused a moment before answering, as if assessing how she felt. "No."

"Can you move your fingers for me?"

She did so, and he nodded. She seemed to be breathing okay. "So, nothing hurts besides your shoulder? No throbbing or tingling anywhere?"

"Just feeling a little stunned. But only my shoulder hurts." Madison took a deep breath.

He fought a grin. "Yeah, you keep saying that. You sure you didn't hit your head?"

She blinked at him. "Oh. Sorry. Can I sit up now?"

He agreed, and she sat up, clutching her shoulder. Bits of grass hay, dirt and chaff clung to her pale blue shirt. "Let me have a look at that shoulder."

Once she was upright, her worried expression slid to the barn where the hands were pulling the horses out. They were locking them up in a corral several yards from the barn. The sirens whined in the distance.

Briggs began to ask her more questions while he gently probed the back side of her right shoulder, careful not to use too much pressure while he checked for potential fractures and other issues.

She answered his questions slowly, occasionally sucking in a sharp breath at his examination. He was being as gentle as he could, but it didn't matter. Her shoulder felt square and her arm hung limply beside her.

"I think you've dislocated your shoulder. Did you try to catch yourself on that arm as you fell?" Briggs knew she wasn't going to like his diagnosis.

"Um, yeah, I think so." Madison wore a scared expression again. She likely expected his next statement.

"I'm going to need to put it back into place." Briggs looked into her eyes, noticing how beautiful they were, despite the poor timing for noting such things. A beautiful shade of green, they shone at him like rare jewels.

She nodded. "I was afraid of that." She glanced at the door. "You don't think he'll come back, do you?"

He followed her gaze. "It's hard to say."

The fear in her expression didn't ease any. "Do we have time to do this right now? Or should we get to the house?"

She was shaking now. Briggs wanted to ease her fear and pain, but it was going to hurt worse before it was better. "I'd rather not wait. The sooner it's put back into place, the less lasting damage will be done. Madison, I'm sorry. This isn't going to be easy for you, but I have no doubt you are tough enough to handle it. You are still a country girl, even if you've been living in the city. Country girls are tougher than most."

His words brought a shaky smile to her face. "Can you just do it and get it over with?"

He chuckled. "Okay, then."

Briggs felt around, finding the right grip. He had only done this once before, under the direction of a superior officer, but he remembered it well.

"Take a deep breath." He gave the instruction to Madison, and then with a quick jerk, it was done. She shrieked and then fell silent, sucking in deep breaths.

"That wasn't so bad." She tried for lightness, but her face was pale. "Let's go find the perp."

Briggs frowned at her. "Not a chance. You need pain relievers, ice and rest. You're going to be sore."

To his dismay, her eyes filled with tears. "How long?"

Briggs wasn't sure what she meant. "How long do you need to rest? Or how long will you be sore?"

"No." She shook her head. "How long will this person get away with tormenting me? Why can't we catch him? Or her. Whoever."

Briggs ached for her. The physical pain she was in probably only served as an aggravation to the emotional anxiety she was feeling.

"Not long. I'll see to that. I promise I'll keep you safe until we catch him."

Madison couldn't control her shaking. She was relieved when Briggs settled her on the couch back in the house, plying her with pain relievers, water, an ice pack and a blanket. "Is this what they mean by shock? I can't stop shaking."

Briggs bent his long legs and sat in a chair close by after reading something on his phone. "Maybe a mild bit of shock. Your body had quite a rush of adrenaline there, along with a painful injury. You're just coming down from it."

He was kind. Patient. She hadn't expected such gentleness from this man. He looked strong, tough, but he treated her with so much respect.

Her father and Adria were both sleeping, so they hadn't told them what had happened. Mrs. Newman, determined to be there despite the danger, was preparing dinner, and the house was otherwise quiet. Briggs had told Mrs. Newman that they could manage until it was safe. But she'd declared the people on the ranch to be the closest thing she had to family and staunchly refused to stay at home.

Madison suddenly felt very alone with Briggs. The weight of his attention on her made her a little self-conscious. It only intensified when he leaned over and pulled a piece of straw from her hair.

"And the horses are all out okay. The fire didn't seem to do too much damage. The hands are going to let me know when they know more." He sat back, rolling the piece of straw between his fingers. "You're going to want to shower as soon as you feel up to it. That hay is going to get itchy in a hurry."

It occurred to her she was probably getting his sofa all dirty as well. "I'm sorry, Briggs. I shouldn't be on your furniture."

He stopped her when she started to rise. "Stay put. It's fine. It can be cleaned. Just relax until you feel up to it." He thought for a moment. "I can run you a bath if you'd rather."

The idea of a warm bath sounded absolutely amazing. Madison's apartment was small and only had a shower, so it had been some time since she had indulged in a nice long soak.

She nodded. "Honestly, that sounds really great. But if you'll show me the way, I can run my own water."

He shook his head, rising from the chair. "I think you'd better give it a few minutes. I'll let you know when it's ready, and I'll help you to the bathroom, just to be sure. As soon as I get you settled with a bath,

I need to go update the sheriff's deputy. Maybe he saw something that would give us a clue. I'm not sure how someone is coming and going without being seen."

"Of course. I hope he can help." She watched him leave to go fill the tub. She didn't feel like she needed that much help with the bath, but his pampering was nice, to be sure. When he returned to get her, she entered the master bathroom to find he had filled the tub with bubbles, laid out a fluffy towel and thick robe, and even lit a few candles near the tub.

When she looked at him, his face turned a little pink. "You've had a tough day. It won't hurt to relax a bit. I hope this might help get your mind off everything."

She smiled. "I don't know what to say. This is amazing. Thank you."

"You're welcome." He nodded before ducking out the door.

Madison ended her relaxing bath feeling refreshed and renewed. After dressing in some comfy clothes, she returned to the living room to find her father and

Adria had both awakened in her absence. They were listening intently as Briggs relayed the details of the incident in the barn to them.

Adria rushed toward Madison as soon as she entered. "Oh, Madi! Briggs was just telling us about what happened in the barn. I'm so glad you're okay."

Her friend put an arm around her and led her to a chair, settling her before she said any more. "I just don't know how you are holding up so well. I would be an absolute wreck in your place."

Her father looked concerned, too. "What can we do, Briggs? We've gotta do something soon or Madison is going to be seriously injured."

Briggs pondered his question for a moment. "I'm working on a plan, but until I figure out the details, it's best Madison stays close to me at all times."

Adria squeezed Madison in a tight hug, careful to stay on the side away from her injured shoulder. "I'm so glad you have Briggs watching out for you. I feel much better about your safety just meeting him. Honestly, I was going to beg you to come back to Boston, but now that I've met Briggs, I'm not so sure about that."

Madison nodded in wholehearted agreement. She definitely did feel much better knowing Briggs was nearby. "He has been great."

Briggs clenched his strong jaw, face flushing a bit, and shook his head. "I'm only human. You still need to always be on your guard. And pray. Definitely pray."

Conversation turned to other things, but Madison's attention went to Briggs. What was it about him that made her feel so safe and secure? True, he was still strong and muscular from his days as a SEAL and the continuous ranch work, but it was something much deeper than just his physical strength. It was something in his character.

Adria was studying her carefully, and she surprised Madison with a knowing smile. No telling what her friend was going to accuse her of later. She shook her head at Adria, sending a slight eye roll her way.

Mrs. Newman appeared from the kitchen. "Dinner will be ready in about five minutes. I am taking the roast from the oven."

"Is that what that delicious smell is?" Adria sent her a charming smile. "I can't wait to taste it."

Madison nodded in agreement. "My mouth has been watering for a half hour, for sure."

Briggs looked at Jake. "Would you show Adria to the table? I'd like to talk to Madison for just a moment."

Jake nodded, and Adria's eyes widened, but she didn't say anything. When they had disappeared, Briggs pulled Madison close. "I heard back from Avery while you were in the bath. He thinks this might be related to one of your stories from a few months ago. Do you recall the murder involving a musician's brother? It's a cold case that re-emerged after the singer gained notoriety. He wanted to reopen it to see if the murder could be solved."

Madison made a noise of agreement. "Yes, I remember. As far as I know, no new evidence ever came to light. The musician was pretty disappointed with the outcome."

"Well, someone hasn't let it go. When Avery was looking at your article, the database linked another, more recent article. Sources said the case has been reopened at the behest of the musician. It mentioned your original article and he thinks there is a possibility that whoever is behind the murder has seen it."

Madison pressed her lips together, thinking. "You think someone is angry at me for bringing attention back to the case?"

"It's our strongest lead so far. The problem is, since the murder is unsolved, we don't have anywhere to start. All we have is the victim's name." Briggs glanced toward the kitchen when Adria laughed at something someone had said. "I know I'm probably being too cautious, but maybe the less said in front of your friend the better right now. I'm sure she wouldn't intentionally do anything to jeopardize the investigation, but if she accidentally mentioned something to the wrong person from your office, it could make it harder to figure this whole thing out. There seems to be a link somewhere."

"You're right. It is probably best to keep it as quiet as possible for a little while." Madison looked toward the kitchen, feeling a bit guilty for not being there with Adria and her father. "I'll pull my research from the story and get it to you. Maybe there is something that could help."

"Avery is doing a thorough check on it, but if we could send him what you have, it might help." Briggs gestured toward the kitchen. "We'd better join them. We can discuss it more later. I just wanted you to know in case you can think of something."

"Of course. Thank you." Madison stood, but before she walked into the kitchen, she turned to Briggs. "Thank you again. I don't know how I would have made it through today without you."

He looked a little uncomfortable, but he smiled. "Don't thank me yet."

SEVEN

Briggs knew Avery's theory made sense, but for some reason, he didn't feel like it was quite right. He fully intended to do all he could to follow up on it, but after dinner tonight, he planned to skim through Madison's recent articles to search for clues.

He observed quietly as Madison and Adria engaged in easy conversation over the delicious meal Mrs. Newman had prepared. He interjected an occasional comment, as did Jake, but for the most part, the women carried the conversation. Briggs had never been that talkative, nor was Jake. Many nights they ate in silence, both completely comfortable with that.

He only half listened to the conversation as he replayed the recent attacks in his mind. None of them held any real clues about who could be behind them.

If anyone besides Jake noticed how distracted Briggs was, they didn't comment on it. He did, however, notice his foreman watching him a time or two, and he didn't for a second think Jake was oblivious to his thoughts. The old man's questioning gaze led Briggs to believe that Jake was anxious to talk about the events of the day.

Truthfully, Briggs would much rather be hashing out the details instead of sitting here eating a nice dinner and pretending nothing was wrong. Madison seemed to be soothed by Adria's presence, so he was willing to temper his own desires to do things differently if it meant giving her some relief. She had certainly had enough go wrong for her lately. Briggs couldn't help thinking she was holding up remarkably well.

Adria captured his attention with a question. She was gracious enough to say his name first so he could refocus his attention.

"Briggs, Madi says you are a former

navy SEAL. You seem young to be retired. How did you manage to escape so soon?" Adria leaned forward as if fascinated by the thought.

"I received an honorable discharge." He didn't comment further.

"Really?" She sounded even more fascinated, and he wished she would drop it. Instead, she placed her delicate chin on a folded knuckle. He felt sure she knew he didn't want to discuss it, yet she was behaving as if he didn't mind at all.

He simply nodded, and she shook her head. "I really want to hear the story. I'm not letting you off the hook that easily."

He felt his jaw clench. "I don't really talk about what happened in the SEALs to strangers." He stole a glance at Madison, who looked a little guilty. Did she feel bad that her friend had asked the question? Or did she think him rude to refuse to answer Adria?

He was surprised when Adria let it drop. "Tell me about the ranch, then. Not many people are brave enough to raise bison."

Briggs shrugged. "These are pretty much domesticated. It's not much different than raising regular cattle."

Adria raised a brow. "Oh, really?"

Briggs began to explain to her about the government programs in place for the preservation of the species. "They are a lot like mustangs, except the wild mustangs tend to get overpopulated, whereas buffalo are much more scarce. Diseases like brucellosis are taking chunks out of the few remaining wild buffalo. We do our best to keep them as close to wild as possible, though."

Briggs wasn't sure why, but he was uneasy around Adria. Something about her made him feel like he needed to be careful what he said. Maybe it was just the fact that she was a journalist. He had once had a bad experience with a news reporter taking his words out of context, and he hadn't forgotten it easily. It didn't help that it was about Emily's case.

When his fiancée had been found brutally murdered, he hadn't done much to temper his reaction and should have been much more careful of who was listening. His remarks about wanting to see the man who killed Emily suffer had been widely publicized, and many had felt his grief-filled remarks were extreme. It had been exaggerated in the media to the point that he sounded vicious, though he only wanted to catch her killer. He knew that not all journalists were that way, but it had made him cautious.

Madison and Adria were still discussing the buffalo, but his mind had gone on to other concerns when their meal was interrupted by a knock at the door.

The deputy from the sheriff's department stood on the porch. "I'm sorry to interrupt your dinner, but something's happened."

Briggs took one look at his face and stepped out to close the door behind him. "Go on."

"We found a strange truck parked out on the far south side of your property." The deputy paused, putting his hands on his hips. "There was no one inside, but we found some explosives. Look homemade but pretty good."

"Was there a license plate? Did you find any evidence that someone's coming back?" Briggs had so many questions, he didn't know where to start.

"Truck was reported stolen. The other deputy is keeping watch, but we have reason to believe the perp took some of the explosives with him. There was a half-empty cardboard box stained with accelerant that might have been full before. It was damp near the top. The timing could be a coincidence, but we don't think so. Not sure why someone would park a truck full of explosives out on the edge of the property and just leave it unless you were taking some with you."

"Where? The house?" Briggs wanted to jump from the porch and run around the side of the house to make sure, but he couldn't leave Madison and the others.

"I checked the house when I pulled up. Didn't see anything, but you might want to consider finding somewhere else to go for a little while. Just in case." The deputy was scanning the property as he spoke.

"Not a bad idea. Thanks. I'll check in as soon as we get settled." Briggs ducked back into the house as the deputy stepped off the porch to leave.

Briggs went inside, wondering how he could get everyone out without causing panic. Madison was watching him with a question in her eyes.

"It's not good news. The truck is parked out front. Everybody needs to go and get in it." Briggs gave the directions quietly. Everyone began to rise and make their way to the old ranch truck.

"What's going on?" Jake asked.

Briggs didn't hesitate any longer. "We need to get out of here. There's a possibility there might be explosives in the house."

Madison's stomach lurched.

"I'll explain later. Just go. We need to hurry." Briggs motioned toward the door, making sure Madison's father and Mrs. Newman were coming as well.

Madison grabbed her friend by the hand. "Come on Adria. I don't think you realize how much danger you've just put yourself in."

Adria paled. "No, maybe not."

Madison was too shaken to worry about anything but keeping them all safe. "Come on. If anyone can keep us safe, it's Briggs."

While everyone loaded into one of the ranch work trucks, Briggs checked the vehicle itself. When he leaned in under the vehicle to shine a light under the truck's undercarriage to ensure there were no explosives there, Madison's anxiety kicked up even more.

They were barely settled when Briggs started the truck, put it in Drive and was about to ease out of the driveway.

"What about Mitzi and Frau?" Madison remembered her animals at the last second.

Briggs slammed the truck into Park. "No one move. I'll be right back."

Madison's heart melted just a bit at his willingness to rescue her pets. He could easily have said there wasn't time. He came back out with one in each arm, struggling to hang on to them.

Madison took Frau and let Adria hold Mitzi. The little Pomeranian stood on Adria's lap as if she were bound for a great adventure. The cat, however, was unimpressed, flicking his tail at them all and curling up on Madison where she sat behind the passenger seat.

Even their antics couldn't ease the frantic beating of Madison's heart, though. The thought of anything happening to her family or friends because of her made her nauseous.

Briggs was turning the truck out of the driveway when an explosion echoed across the yard behind them.

Parked next to the house, the truck Madison's father drove had gone up in flames. They could just have easily decided to drive it.

Briggs floored it out of the driveway.

"We're getting out of here until a bomb squad checks this place out."

Madison saw Briggs glance at her in the

rearview mirror, and she could read the concern on his face. She barely made it to Mrs. Newman's house before losing the contents of her stomach. Adria came in to check on her after she had been in the bathroom for a few minutes.

"Are you okay, Madi?" She handed her a washcloth from the shelf beside the sink.

"Not really. I won't be okay until this is over, I'm afraid." Madison took the cloth and wet it under the faucet.

"I thought I might be sick as well. I completely understand. That was so scary." Adria leaned against the counter.

"You should go back to Boston." Madison ran the cloth over her face before looking back at her friend.

Adria considered that a moment. "I'm honestly thinking about it, but I also hate to leave you like this. I'm not usually one to run like a coward when things get tough."

Madison rinsed the rag and folded it before laying it on the counter. She needed to choose her words carefully. "I know. But this isn't just things getting tough. It's putting your life in danger."

Adria nodded. "I'll consider it, but I can't leave tonight, so we'll have to figure something out."

Mrs. Newman did her best to make them comfortable in her modest home, but they were all on edge until Briggs finally got a call giving the all-clear at the Whitson ranch. There would be an investigation, according to the deputy Briggs spoke to, but they could at least all return.

It was growing late when they returned, and though Madison was still pretty tied in knots about the recent events, Adria was yawning.

Adria rose. "I do think I'm going to retire to my room. Do you guys mind?"

Briggs had just returned from another phone call with the sheriff's department, and though he was tight-lipped, Madison knew he had something to tell her.

"No, go ahead. I'm going to try to relax a bit before I do the same, maybe drink some warm herbal tea or something. There's no way I can rest right now." Madison smiled.

Adria grasped her hand as she passed. "I understand. Good night."

When she had disappeared down the hall, Madison turned to Briggs. "What did the sheriff's deputies have to say? Are they closer to finding out anything more about the explosives left in the truck?"

"Not a lot. It seems they have a description of the man who stole the truck, but there isn't much else. Nothing to actually ID him," Briggs began. "Onlookers said there was a car that followed the stolen truck."

Madison's stomach tightened. "That's not good news."

"No. It just keeps getting worse. Whoever is after you seems to have plenty of hired help. Someone is either really desperate or has plenty of resources." Briggs seemed to be puzzling it all over, his expression thoughtful.

"Perhaps we need to dig deeper, but I don't really do a whole lot of socializing or anything outside of work. Adria is one of my few close friends, and I don't know many other people in the city besides those I work with." Madison shrugged.

"It could be a stranger who disliked something you wrote, like with the musicians case Avery is looking into, but I am leaning more in the other direction. I have a gut feeling it's someone you know or at least have frequent contact with. We need to take a close look at all of your coworkers." Briggs grimaced. "I know that isn't easy to hear."

"No." Madison swallowed. "But I guess it makes sense. I just can't understand who it could be."

They began listing the names of her coworkers and neighbors she saw frequently, and Madison told him what she knew about each of them. Briggs took notes and nodded as she spoke.

"I'll get these to Avery, and we'll see what they can dig up." He started to close his notebook when a noise outside the window caught their attention. They both looked toward the window and then back to each other.

"You heard that, too?" Madison's heart rate picked up.

He nodded and jumped to his feet. "Stay here."

Flicking off the light, he moved closer to the glass to peek out. Madison followed and looked over his shoulder. Only the moonless night met her eyes.

"Nothing there?" She spoke in a stage whisper.

"I told you to stay back," Briggs whispered.

"I'm not a dog." Madison giggled.

"No, but—"

There was another noise, and Briggs sprang into action, Glock appearing from his waistband like an extension of his arm. "It's coming from the shed. Stay in the house."

Madison watched him go to the door, her protest following him. "But— Please don't leave me here alone. At least you have a gun."

He paused, glancing at her warily. She wasn't sure if he agreed with her or not, but he waved for her to follow. "Fine. But stay low and stay behind me. If you get shot—"

A sudden blast shook the house.

Madison didn't know which way to move. Had it come from the house or the shed? It was impossible to see from their vantage point in the living room.

"Call 911." Briggs dove out the door.

"Where is the deputy?" Madison asked as she began to dial, sticking close to his heels.

"I'm going to find out." Briggs disappeared before she could say more.

Madison was frozen in indecision. Should she keep following him? Check on her father and Adria? Take cover in case the explosion was just a distraction?

Before she could decide, her father appeared. "Madison, what's going on?"

Adria wasn't far behind him, rubbing at her eyes sleepily. "Is everyone okay? Where's Briggs?"

Before she could answer, the pop of gun-shots sounded outside. Madison immediately fell to the ground, shouting at the others to get down also. Adria shrieked but did as Madison suggested.

Worry for Briggs filled Madison. Was he okay? No more shots sounded, and he didn't reappear. Temptation overtook her, and she was about to go out and check on him when the door opened.

Briggs appeared, and relief swept through her. "You're okay!"

"Yes, but Reid, the deputy, was hit. He's pretty badly injured. We have a man in custody. I just called Dispatch, but I could use a hand with Reid. He isn't in such good shape."

Madison didn't ask further questions and followed him out. The first thing she noticed was the flaming shed, but it represented little in the way of urgency with a man's life at risk. Briggs led her to the edge of the porch and past a skinny man cuffed and waiting for someone to take him into custody. He spat curse words at them as soon as he saw them.

"We'll deal with you later. I have no sympathy for you after you shot a deputy," Briggs informed him. The man growled in response.

Madison didn't recognize him. "Who hired you?" She made the demand without thinking. "Why are you here?"

He simply glared at her in return.

"Leave it to the detectives." Briggs gently prodded her. "We need to take care of Reid."

The deputy was lying against a tree in the front yard, a makeshift bandage pressed against his shoulder. It didn't appear to be doing a lot of good judging by the amount of blood covering his arm. His face was pale, even in the low light.

"Good thing he's a poor shot," he joked.

"Not poor enough." Briggs shook his head at him. "You're losing a lot of blood."

The deputy closed his eyes. "I'm more worried about the fire in my shoulder.

Could someone put that out? Call the fire department."

Madison had to admire his spunk, striving for humor at a time like this. "Let me have a look. I know a little basic first aid. At least maybe we can keep some of that blood in your body. I don't know that I can squelch the fire. No training in firefighting."

He gave her a weak grin and released his grip on the shoulder. "I like her, Briggs. If she decides she's too good for you, I wanna be the first to know."

Briggs grunted at him. "You're talking nonsense, Reid."

The deputy tried for a laugh, but it came out pained. Madison examined the wound quickly and nodded at Briggs. "Lie all the way down for me, deputy." She turned to Briggs. "If we can keep pressure on this artery and slow the blood flow, he'll be in better shape. There's no way to tie it off with where the wound is located, but if you can hold it here, I can keep pressure on the wound itself."

Briggs put pressure on the spot she indicated. She had the deputy hold the old bandage on his wound until she could figure out a new bandage. Briggs wore a T-shirt under his button-down, so he offered the extra shirt as a clean covering.

"You owe me a new shirt, Reid," he teased the deputy, hoping to keep him alert.

Reid nodded and closed his eyes. "Just make sure I live to pay up."

"I suspect the bullet is still lodged in his shoulder somewhere. I can't get a good look with all the blood." Madison spoke the words softly to Briggs.

"Most likely so. There doesn't seem to be an exit wound, but thankfully, it's in the meaty part of his shoulder." There was teasing in his voice.

"I can still hear you, you know." Reid opened one eye.

"I hope so. Good thing you've been working out." Briggs frowned at him.

"Won't be again until this heals." The deputy scowled.

"It should heal quickly with good medical care." Madison made a sympathetic face. "How did this happen?"

Reid winced. "He wasn't smart enough to just leave after setting the explosives. A lot of times, arsonists and explosive experts want to hang around to see their work. I saw him moving in the shadows, but he saw me, too. He shot before Briggs could cover me."

The sirens became audible in the distance at that moment. "It's a good thing for you that they must have the speedy paramedics on call tonight." Briggs watched the lights coming up the drive. The driver silenced the sirens, but the red and yellow flashing continued.

Blue and red lights tailed them, indicating the officers had also arrived. When the paramedics took over for them, Briggs stepped away to see about the captured man. Madison stood there in uncertainty, watching the scene unfold.

Reid caught her attention, however, as the paramedics injected some pain reliever into his IV and prepared to load him in the truck. "Thank you. I appreciate your help more than you know."

Madison smiled at him in return. "Thank you, but it was nothing. It's my fault you took a bullet to begin with."

He lay back against the gurney as the pain killers went to work. "Just doing my job, ma'am. All in a day's work."

She laughed softly. "I hope not."

But he was out.

EIGHT

After watching the church service the next day, Briggs decided he was going to have to change his plans for bringing in the buffalo herd. Severe storms were predicted for the upcoming week, and he didn't want the bison left in the far pasture where they were now, miles from the house. He had planned on rotating them to a nearby pasture until the spring weather passed, but that had been put off because of more pressing things.

He hadn't slept much the night before, his thoughts consumed with the attacks. He had wanted badly to question the skinny man they had apprehended before the police took him into custody, but he knew better than to interfere. Had the man simply been trying to eliminate Madison's protection, or was there a greater plan at work? With more than one person involved, it was hard to guess. And how had they known the bomb squad had already finished their sweep of the property? Were there people watching their every move?

He had wrapped up the report with law enforcement as quickly as he could and gotten Madison back inside. Paramedics had taken Reid to the nearest hospital, and another deputy had been dispatched to take his place. But this definitely wasn't over just yet.

Briggs really needed to move the buffalo herd, though, and the sooner the better. When he explained the situation to Madison, she nodded. "I'll need you to ride out with us but stay out of the way."

"Why? I can help. You'll be a man short without my father, anyway. Your horses are trained to work the buffalo herd, right?" She cocked her head to the side and waited.

"Well, yeah. But what about you? It's been a while since you've worked on a

ranch, much less with these huge beasts."
Briggs shook his head.

"I think I can handle it. I rode out with
you the other day with no problems. It
comes back quickly."

Briggs sighed. "Yes, but working cattle,
or bison, in this case, is a little more chal-
lenging than just going for a ride. And no
doubt that shoulder is very sore."

"I am aware of that. How about I just let
you know if I start to feel it's too much?
You could use the help. And I'd really like
to be useful. A couple of ibuprofen and I'll
be fine." Madison stared him down.

Briggs threw up his hands. "Okay. We
can try it. But if at any time you feel afraid
or out of control in the least, I want you to
just back off and let us handle it, okay?"

She nodded, grinning triumphantly.

Briggs called Lance, the cowhand he
had appointed temporary foreman during Jake's convalescence, and told him to
gather the men. The Whitsons had rebuilt
the main house over two decades before
when a fire had all but destroyed most of

the original home. The new location was a pretty good ways from the bunkhouse, and the old structure still haunted the land near where the hands slept. Wade had once told him they hadn't had the heart to tear it down. Briggs probably never would, either.

By the time they had the horses saddled and rode out, Madison's expression turned to one of pure joy. It was apparent she loved riding and ranch work. Briggs wondered why she had moved to the city. When he'd introduced her to the hands, she'd remembered several of them from growing up in the area. Was there something here she wanted to avoid? He had no idea who or what it could be, for everyone seemed to think well of her.

She rode next to a hand by the name of Clancy. He was probably around her age, and they talked in an animated way as the posse made their way to the far pasture to round up the bison. She had mentioned remembering Clancy from their childhood when Briggs had told her the hand's name. Briggs tried to remind himself it wasn't any of his concern, but he still wondered what they could be talking about. No doubt it was just a shared memory, but he couldn't temper the desire to be a part of the conversation.

Madison glanced in his direction and smiled. He nodded and looked away, hoping she didn't think too much of him watching her and would just assume it was because he wanted to keep her safe. He did, but there was definitely more to it. It had been quiet around the ranch since all the excitement the night before, but Briggs knew the attacks weren't over. To the contrary, he felt in his gut stronger than ever that the person behind the attacks was still at large.

The ride out to the far pasture was long and gave Briggs too much time to think about the past and why he didn't want to be having these feelings for Madison. They went far beyond protectiveness and worry over how he was going to keep her safe.

He didn't really want to think about his past romance, but more than that, he didn't want to ever take that kind of risk again. Loving someone and losing them was the worst pain he had ever experienced in his life.

When the bison finally came into view in the distance, Briggs knew it was time to refocus his attention on the task at hand, at least temporarily. Not giving these huge beasts his full attention could be deadly.

The wooly creatures looked peaceful and serene grazing on the sloping plain, but though the bison could be gentle enough at times, their sheer size alone was dangerous. Some weighed in at well over a ton, and if frightened, they could easily trample a person to death. They certainly had in the annals of history.

As the riders drew nearer, he pulled his gelding up alongside Madison's horse and began to give her instructions. "I want you to stay close to me. We can work together at swing. I'm going to let Lance take point just in case any issues arise."

Madison nodded and smiled, looking happy and content to be working on a ranch again. He knew from stories he had heard from her and her father, as well as memories Wade had shared with him about Chop, that she had once been quite a hand with a horse before she moved off to college and became a journalist.

He shouldn't be so curious about her history, but he would love to know just what had convinced her to leave this behind and move to the city. He could understand wanting to leave a place when too many bad memories awaited you there, but he also knew that sometimes those memories had to be reconciled to move on in life.

The hands began to circle the herd and gently prod them into moving forward in the right direction. They wasted no time, since it would likely be well past dark before they got them back to the pasture near the house. Beating the storms would be the main concern. Already he could see the tall pillars of clouds forming high in the sky, dark shadows creeping up on them from a distance. The storms weren't predicted to arrive in the area until after dark, but even the best meteorologist had little ability to predict Oklahoma weather. Nothing was ever certain here, and an unexpected tornado could not only scatter the herd but also wreak all kinds of havoc on lives and landscapes.

The bison were docile despite the coming storms. He knew that could change in an instant, though, so he reminded everyone to stay vigilant.

Madison was close enough to talk to, and when the herd continued to stay calm, she started up a conversation.

"The herd has grown so much. They look healthy and strong. You're doing a great job with them." She continued to look them over as she spoke.

"The Whitsons did the hard work. I have just been maintaining what they built. Miranda has been a great teacher. I didn't know much about bison when she handed over the workings of the ranch."

It took longer to move the herd than Briggs had expected, and when the sky began to change, the herd grew restless.

Briggs eyed the ominous clouds and called out a few commands to the hands. It was getting dark, not only because of the impending sunset. The clouds were taking on a deep steely gray cast as well.

"We're going to have to push them a little harder. We might not have as much time as we thought," Briggs said as he assessed the landscape. The ranch house was in sight, but with the flat, treeless range ahead of them, that didn't mean a lot.

The herd adjusted to the increase in pace fine for a little bit, and Briggs was beginning to think it would work. Without warning, however, one of the bull calves broke away and tore across the field between two flank riders, bucking, kicking and snorting. A cowboy rode out after him, but the mama cow became frantic. The animals around her began to snort and toss their heads as well.

"Slow them down! We have to get them calmed," Briggs shouted, and the point riders made their move. The herd didn't respond at first, but when the cowboy who had gone out after the calf drove him back, the mother sniffed her baby and settled.

Briggs breathed a sigh of relief, and he sent up a prayer of thanks that they had been able to calm the herd so quickly.

Madison, too, was looking a little pale. He noticed her eyeing the herd in awe when they had started out earlier. They were a little intimidating up close, even to those accustomed to working with bison.

He wanted to ease her mind, so he rode up alongside her. "I thought I was about to see your champion riding skills in action. You might have to do some trick riding to ease my disappointment."

"Oh, that would be entertaining, for sure. You would be picking me up off the ground." She giggled. "I thought I would try some of those tricks once as a child. I wound up with a broken arm and two fractured ribs."

Briggs raised a brow and widened his eyes at her. "Ouch. I guess that was the end of your trick riding career."

"My dad informed me it wasn't the sort

of skill that was self-taught, and if I wanted to learn, he would get me lessons." Madison laughed. "He was being facetious, of course."

"I can imagine Jake saying that and not making a big deal of your injuries." Briggs grinned.

"He was always one of those 'rub some dirt on it and keep going' kind of fathers, for sure. He didn't really handle crying well." Madison had barely finished the sentence when lightning flared across the sky followed by a rumble of thunder. She jumped slightly.

"That sounded awfully close." Briggs glanced around.

One of the hands across the herd adjusted his hat and whistled long and slow as he spoke to one of the cowboys near him. The herd was becoming restless and jumpy again.

"Maybe it was just a stray bolt. If we stay calm, the herd will as well." Briggs issued the statement as a stiff wind kicked up.

Darkness had fallen on them like a curtain, swift and suddenly. Madison shivered. They were running out of time. They needed to finish this job and get to some cover.

Briggs and the other hands went to work as a cohesive unit, pushing the bison as fast as they dared toward the pasture where the herd would be kept through the spring. Madison was a good hand and helped as much as the seasoned men.

Briggs didn't miss the relief that colored her face, even in the darkness, when he indicated the pasture they would turn the bison into was just ahead. He felt that same relief, but it was short-lived.

When they had the gate in sight, Madison pulled her horse back, putting some distance between her mare and the herd to allow the cowboys some space to push the bison through the gate without spooking them. Briggs was prepared to direct her, but Madison didn't need it. Briggs had no doubt she had done this before. She made the adjustments smoothly, as if it was a natural instinct.

Just as they were making the turn with the bison at the gate that was the symbol of victory, a thundering began that had nothing to do with the coming storm. A ripple of horror went through Briggs. He had no doubt it was the noise of a stampede. What he didn't know was what had caused it. He didn't have time to ponder that, though. He was too busy worrying about the stampeding herd heading straight for Madison.

NINE

Terror filled Madison as realization sank in.

The entire herd, probably more than fifty buffalo, was headed straight for her. She kicked Kat into motion, leaning over the mare's neck to urge her to use every ounce of speed she possessed. The mare responded with grit, seemingly aware of the urgency of the situation.

The darkness camouflaged the ground, making it impossible to tell if dark splotches were gopher holes or clumps of grass between lightning flashes. Heedless of the danger, the mare ate up the ground while Madison prayed she didn't step into a hole. Visions of the mare snapping a leg as she tumbled breakneck into the path of a herd of stampeding bison fought for headspace as she tried to concentrate on finding a route away from the runaway beasts.

She could hear Briggs shouting above the thunder, directing the hands in a desperate attempt to contain the massive herd. Rain started then, too, blowing with the wind and pelting her in stinging lashes across her face. Ducking her head as much as she dared, she turned the mare in a far-reaching arc away from the path of the stampede. She prayed the buffalo wouldn't follow. If she could get out of their path, maybe the animals would just run themselves into a lather and slow down on their own.

She dared a glance over her shoulder. Her mare was fast, and the herd was cumbersome, giving her an advantage, but there was a rocky slope just ahead. She was going to have to slow her mare or risk serious injury to them both. She would have to take the chance.

She pulled up her mare, slowing as much as she dared, hoping she could get past the rough patch without the herd catching up. It began to hail as the storm intensified.

Lighting flared, too close and accompanied by an earth-rattling boom, and Kat squealed in panic. Before Madison could react, the mare reared onto her hind legs, sending Madison sliding from the saddle.

She fought to hang on, but her balance had shifted. Clinging desperately to the saddle horn, Madison used every bit of strength she had to maintain her grip. As the mare settled, she pulled with all her might, trying to reseat herself in the saddle. Pellets of hail pounded at her as she tried to get leverage. The rain had made her grip slippery, and it wasn't enough. She tried for calm as her hands slid, and before she could recover, another flashing boom had her mare dancing and rearing again. Madison couldn't maintain her grip.

She slid from the horse's back, landing in a crumpled heap on the ground. With little time to register the rumbling of the ground below her, she shot up and took off on foot. She knew she couldn't outrun the herd, so she prayed with every ounce of energy she had left for any kind of intervention.

Madison didn't bother to look back to see how close the herd was. She stumbled a few times over the deepening spring grass and slippery quarter-sized hail, fighting for breath as her lungs made as much effort as her legs. The intensity of the rumbling on the ground beneath her kept her well apprised of the growing nearness of the wooly beasts behind her. She tried to swallow back the fear clawing at her even as the hail blistered her.

This was it.

She didn't know how she was going to come out of this alive. Madison was suddenly aware that the hoofbeats close by were different. Just as the thought registered, a strong arm swept her up tightly. Briggs swung her up, and she landed just behind the saddle.

"Grab hold!" Briggs had to shout to be heard over the cacophony of noise around them. The wind swirled rain all around them, and the sound of thunder and hoofbeats fought for dominance. The howling wind suddenly stilled for an instant, then a low, mournful sound like a lonely freight train filled the darkened night.

"Twister," one of the hands bellowed from somewhere far to their right.

"We've gotta get out of here." Briggs issued the command over the eerie sound.

Madison took a deep breath and hung on to Briggs as he dug his calves into the gelding's sides, and they took off. The breath of the stampeding bison seemed to heat her legs as the horse cleared the path mere seconds before the bison.

She didn't have time to sigh with relief, though, for as the lightning continued to strike, she could see the tornado bearing down on them as well. It wasn't large, but it was dangerous just the same. The hail continued, growing larger by the second as it swirled up and down in the atmosphere.

The barn was still a far distance off and didn't offer any protection from a tornado, so Briggs urged the horse toward the pond.

There was a dry gulch along one side of it. He helped her from the saddle, and Briggs tossed the reins over his gelding's neck and gave him a slap to send him running to the barn. He would be better off seeing to his own safety once he didn't have two people to carry. Briggs and Madison hustled to flatten themselves into the mud behind the embankment.

The smell of damp dirt filled Madison's flaring nostrils. She hadn't yet caught her breath, and the adrenaline still pulsing through her system wasn't doing much to remedy the problem. Briggs breathed hard beside her, too, and when she looked up, their eyes met.

"Are you okay?" His gaze ran the length of her, checking for anything out of the ordinary.

Madison nodded. "So far. I'll be better when we get out of this storm."

"Same here." Briggs pressed his lips tightly together. "Stay low. It's almost on us."

The intensity of the noise barreling down

on them did indeed grow closer, but then it suddenly began to disperse. Briggs risked a glance when the next lightning bolt struck.

"It's losing strength. It turned and hooked back away from us. Stay down, though, just in case." He ducked his head again.

"I hope everyone is okay. Your men…" Madison was leery of elaborating. There was no doubt the hands knew what to do in the event of a tornado, but there weren't a lot of low places to hide out here, and there was a stampeding herd of bison to deal with as well.

Briggs nodded. "I hope so, too. Just keep praying."

She wasn't sure how he knew she had been praying, but she nodded in response. She had a feeling he had been, too.

Madison slowly became aware of aching in various parts of her body. It seemed forever before Briggs helped her up out of the mud. The storm slowed to a steady rain as the winds died away and the thunder grew distant. Even the lightning now faded into the distance.

"Thank You, Lord," Madison whispered as she realized they were okay.

"I'll second that," Briggs said. "We'll head back to the barn. Everyone will meet back up there and see if we are all accounted for. The horses will find their way back there, too."

Madison had guessed as much. Now they had quite a trek ahead of them in the dark, rainy night.

As they emerged from beneath the embankment, she noticed the herd scattered out around them, now wandering calmly in the open pasture. It was still very dark, but she could see their massive shadows rising here and there on the flat plain. The horses had probably made for shelter, and from the looks of things, they'd taken their riders with them. It was quiet all around them, with nothing but the drizzle stirring in the night.

"I guess we're the only ones left out here," Madison commented into the empty darkness.

Briggs remained silent for a moment. "Let's hope that's a good thing."

They started the hike back to the barn, wet denim clinging to her legs and chilling her in the cool, post-thunderstorm air, and Madison shivered involuntarily.

"I wish I had something warm and dry to offer you. Maybe if we pick up the pace, we'll warm up. Can you keep up?" He gestured out in front of them.

"I'll do my best." Madison gave him a smile, but it felt weak.

They had been walking for a several long minutes along the trail the animals and vehicles had cut through the fields when the faint glow of headlights came at them in the distance.

Madison froze.

In all the excitement from the stampede and the storm, she had forgotten about her pursuer.

Until now.

Briggs tensed when he saw the headlights. He stopped, too, and turned to her.

"I'm sure it's just some of the hands coming to look for us. Hopefully, the tornado drove your attacker underground for a bit." To be honest, he wasn't really sure anymore, and after the night they had had so far, anything seemed possible. Despite the storm, he had his suspicions about what had really caused the herd to stampede. His bison were usually even-tempered and docile.

She gave a little nod and started walking again, but he could sense she was tense and poised to run. He kept his guard up as well.

"It's Dad and one of the hands," Madison said, exhaling as the vehicle drew closer. "Thank You, Lord."

Briggs silently echoed her sentiment.

The white dually pulled up beside them and stopped. A hand named Stockton rolled down the driver's side window and peered out. Jake leaned in from the passenger side. Both men uttered a declaration of thanks.

"We thought y'all got caught out in the

tornado," Stockton said. His young face showed obvious relief.

"We sort of did. But we hid out under the embankment by the old pond until it blew over. Thankfully, it went around us. How are the rest of the hands? Anyone injured?" Briggs asked, looking over Stockton's lanky frame behind the truck door. He had a boyish look about him, and one long, skinny arm hung out the window.

"We all made it back to the barn ahead of the tornado. It turned back the other direction before it got to us. Everyone's fine." He motioned for them to get into the truck. "Y'all look like you could use a ride in. Maybe we can hash out the details once everyone is dry."

Briggs helped Madison into the back seat and jumped in behind her. She apologized for getting the seat wet.

"It's a work truck, ma'am. It'll be fine." Stockton gave a little chuckle.

She was always worried about little niceties, even when everything was going wrong. Her pinched brow proved she was

still concerned, despite Stockton's reas-
surances.

"The herd looks to be okay from what
I can tell in the darkness. We'll have to
round them all up again in the morning."
Briggs was talking to the men, but his
thoughts were still on Madison.

"Yeah, Lance is already getting everyone briefed on that." Stockton dodged a
pothole in the field that Jake pointed out.

"Good. Hopefully, none of them will get
too far before morning. Any damage to
the ranch?" Briggs gripped the seat back
in front of him as the truck swayed with
another swerve.

"One of the hands called while we were
driving out. The bunkhouse had a little damage to the roof, but nothing too
bad. Also, the barn got some hail damage. Hopefully, we won't find any leaks."
Stockton ran down a list of smaller things,
like downed trees.

"It certainly could have been worse.
Maybe the worst of it missed us." Briggs
blew out a breath.

They were soon back at the house, and Madison wearily climbed from the back seat, reminding Briggs that she was probably hurting all over from the fall as well as the relentless hail. He offered her some assistance getting into the house, but Stockton called out to him before he could get inside.

When Briggs turned, he noticed deep concern etched onto Stockton's face.

"Sir, I'd like to talk to you about something I saw."

A knot of concern formed in Briggs's midsection. "What did you see, Stockton?"

The cowboy hesitated. "I know this is gonna sound silly, especially with all the other things that went on tonight. But I think you should know."

Briggs nodded, trying to encourage the young cowboy. "Nothing you feel I need to know is too insignificant to tell me now."

Stockton stared at his boots. "It's about the stampede that happened just before the storm. Those buffalo were just fine. There was no reason for them to spook like that when they did."

Briggs rolled his shoulders back, glancing at Madison, who was about to step through the door to go in. "Buffalo, like cattle, can easily spook out of nowhere. It's hard to know why they freak out like that sometimes."

"No, sir, you don't understand. I know what it was that caused them to spook. I saw it happen. I don't know who it was, sir, but one of the hands caused that stampede."

"What do you mean someone caused it? How?" Briggs braced his hands on his hips.

Stockton winced. "I saw someone hit several of them with a Hot-Shot. He started the stampede with the cattle prod on purpose."

TEN

A slow anger began to rise within Briggs at the cowhand's words. He fought back the surge of anger as Stockton continued.

"Once he shocked a few of them, the others started to panic, too, and then next thing I knew, they were stampeding. I couldn't do anything to stop it. I was riding toward the cowboy with the Hot-Shot, but I was too late. He disappeared into the melee when the herd scattered." Stockton shrugged. "I couldn't tell who it was."

"Did you find the Hot-Shot?" Briggs was referring to the long, stick-like object that emitted electrical shocks. Not many ranchers used them anymore because they weren't necessary to get domesticated cattle to move, but they were still available. Briggs didn't like them.

"No, I didn't see it. Could be he tossed it. Maybe we'll find it when we round the herd up tomorrow." Stockton looked uncomfortable, shifting from foot to foot.

"Is there more?" Briggs asked, thinking Stockton might be hedging.

"No, sir, that's all, except I'm sorry I couldn't do more. And I'm glad the lady's all right." He nodded and ducked off toward the bunkhouse.

"Thank you," Madison called out after him. He glanced back toward her and nodded once again.

When the cowhand was gone, Briggs hustled her on into the house before she could question him further, but he knew she wouldn't be put off once they were inside.

"One of your ranch hands? How could this happen? What connection could any of them have to someone in Boston?" Madison wore a stricken expression.

"We don't know that it was actually

one of my hands. It was dark. Someone could have snuck in on horseback and pretended to be one of the hands long enough to spook the bison." Briggs considered the possibility aloud.

"You don't think the other hands would have noticed a stranger?" Madison glanced at her father.

"I don't know, but I fully intend to find out what's going on. As soon as I change clothes, I'm going to the bunkhouse to question the hands." Briggs motioned down the hall. "I think you should take a hot bath. You should be safe enough here with your father and the deputy outside while I'm gone, and you need to get some rest."

Jake was nodding, but Madison shook her head. "I want to go with you. Don't I have a right to hear what they have to say?"

Briggs nodded. "Of course you do. I just thought you'd rather warm up and rest. But I'll wait on you here in the living room after I've changed clothes."

He should know by now she wasn't the kind of woman who would want to just hide out and stay comfortable while he did the legwork.

He put on a dry pair of work jeans and a fresh T-shirt and dug out a pair of old boots from the back of his closet. He towel-dried his damp hair before running his fingers through the loose strands. He went to the kitchen to find Mrs. Newman had wisely anticipated their need for hot coffee and poured some into a couple of insulated cups from a cabinet near the coffee station. When he came out of the kitchen, he met Madison and handed her one of the coffees.

"Thank you so much." She gave him a grateful smile.

She had scrubbed her face clean of the light makeup she had worn earlier, and her damp hair was drawn back away from her face in a simple ponytail. It gave her a girl-next-door look that made him wish for things he had no business wishing for—not with her or anyone else. Losing someone hurt too much. He didn't want to go through that again.

He muttered a gruff response and prodded her toward the door. "Let's go. I don't really wanna have to drag them all out of bed to get some answers."

Briggs's whole demeanor had changed when Madison appeared in the hallway. She had no idea what that was about, so she didn't ask. She had checked in on Adria and found she had already gone back to bed after learning everyone was okay. Madison followed Briggs to the UTV he kept in the garage, and they rode out to the bunkhouse. It was a brief and quiet ride, but when he pulled up to the bunkhouse and cut the engine, he looked at her.

"I'd appreciate it if you'd just let me ask the questions. If I suspect any danger, I'll give you a signal, and I want you to run. Get to the barn and lock yourself in the tack room." She noticed he wore the Glock at his hip and shivered. Maybe she should have stayed behind after all.

She nodded and followed him from the UTV. At the door, he called out to let them know she was with them. She supposed a bunkhouse full of men probably didn't pay much attention to their state of dress when they were alone. She was relieved Briggs had thought of it, for she wouldn't have.

The bunkhouse was perfectly neat and clean, much to Madison's surprise. The men looked up at her as she entered and began to congregate at the table at Briggs's behest. There were six of them in total, and they ranged in size, shape and age. She smiled at them all. She already knew some of the men, but Briggs briefly introduced them to her by name.

They waited until all the men were settled around them to begin the discussion. If Stockton was nervous about what he had seen being announced, he didn't let on. He was young and strong, and Madison had no doubts he could handle himself well enough if need be. She breathed in deeply as Briggs cleared his throat.

"I know we have all had a tough night. I

won't keep you up for long since we have a herd of bison to gather up in the morning. There was a reason the herd spooked tonight. What I need to know is whether anyone here saw anything strange before the stampede. I'm sure you are all aware of the fact that someone is out to get Madison. If anyone saw anything, I need you to tell me. Her life could depend on it." Briggs looked around the table at each of the men.

His jaw had hardened, and he had that look—the one Madison thought of as the SEAL expression, the one that gave no quarter. His voice, too, had taken on a different tone. It was harder, more direct. This Briggs was intimidating, harrowing even. Madison was glad he was on her side.

The men began to shift uncomfortably. No one spoke for a few heartbeats as they all gave each other sideways glances.

"I thought there was an extra man out there at one point. I didn't want to sound silly, though, so I kept it to myself. I only noticed because he didn't seem to be doing much, just riding around a lot, but I wasn't close to him and couldn't tell who it was." This came from a short, muscular cowboy named Clint.

"Were you going to mention it to anyone?" Lance asked the question, an edge to his voice.

Clint looked uncomfortable but shrugged. "I didn't really want to get anyone in trouble. When no one else mentioned it, I didn't, either."

Lance frowned at him. "Well, I'd appreciate it if you did so in the future. We have too much to do on the ranch to tolerate that kind of behavior." As foreman in charge while Madison's father was recuperating, Lance was the one the cowboys would report such things to.

Clint nodded. "Yes, sir."

"Now that you mention it, I think I did see that guy. He didn't ride that well, and his horse acted a little funny," one of the older cowboys said. "I was too busy to think much about it at the time."

Lance frowned at Briggs. "I can't believe this."

"It isn't the kind of thing you usually have to worry about while moving a herd. If anyone can give me a description of this fellow, it would sure help." Briggs again looked around the table.

The cowboys again seemed to be silently communicating something, but Madison wasn't sure what it was about. Had they already discussed it amongst themselves? Were they waiting on someone to take the lead?

Finally one of the hands spoke.

"It was pretty dark. He wasn't a big guy. Like Georgie said, he didn't sit a horse particularly well. I couldn't tell much more about him," Clint finally said.

Briggs looked frustrated, but he didn't say anything to that effect to the men. "Okay. Well, if anyone thinks of anything else, let me know as soon as possible. Someone stampeded that herd on purpose, and I need to find out who."

Some of the men gave each other surprised glances, while others nodded as if they knew. A couple of them gave Madison sympathetic looks as well.

By the time they left, several of the men had assured both Madison and Briggs they would be on the lookout for anything that might help solve the mystery of who was behind these attacks. Madison was grateful to have so many strong, loyal men looking out for her. She had never once before thought any of them could be behind the attacks, but now her suspicions grew. What if she was wrong about one of them? What if someone was reporting back to whoever was out to get her?

She felt weary right down to her bones and was more than ready to get into her comfy bed and forget about the latest attack. She was sore, but nothing like she would probably be tomorrow. She followed Briggs out to the UTV and settled in beside him. She paid little attention to their surroundings, however, until Briggs suddenly braked hard and jumped out of the UTV.

"What are you doing?" she asked, unable to keep the weariness from her tone.

Briggs stooped over for a moment before rising again, something small in his hand. "I think I might have found part of the cattle prod."

He held up a plastic-coated metal stick with two vicious-looking metal prongs sticking out from the end. "Looks like it's been broken. Why would the perp discard it here?"

The sharp whir of a passing shot whistled by far too close to them in answer. The report of a rifle soon followed as Briggs shouted at her to get low. He jumped back into the UTV, dropping the broken cattle prod to the floorboard.

"A trap?" Madison couldn't believe how this guy was staying one step ahead of them.

"At the very least, they knew where we were." He launched the UTV into action, slamming them both against the seat back. They ducked as low as they could into the open cab. It offered little protection with only a front and back windshield. The sides were completely open, providing nothing to slow down the shots being fired their way.

The shots kept coming. "How can they see us?"

Briggs shrugged. "Night-vision goggles, I'm sure." He glanced around, keeping his head low. "Get down under the dash as much as you can. I know it isn't much, but it's the best protection we have at the moment." Briggs pointed at the tiny space between the seat and the front of the vehicle.

He was right. It wasn't much, but she complied hastily as another bullet ricocheted off the back fender. Fear for Briggs filled her also.

"Could I have your gun?" Madison was desperate to help. Maybe if she could shoot back, it would deter their attacker somewhat.

They bounced over a particularly deep pothole, and Madison winced as her head glanced off the handle on the side of the UTV.

Briggs sucked in a breath. "Sorry. I

didn't see it. Are you okay?" He spared her a quick glance.

"Yes. Don't worry about me. Just get us out of here." Her voice rose slightly in pitch.

"The Glock won't do you much good right now." He finally addressed her question. "They're too far out of range for a handgun, and my rifles aren't loaded." He waved one hand at a couple of long-range rifles strapped to the back of the UTV. "It's too risky for you to dig out the ammo right now."

"What can I do?" Madison's voice sounded almost shrill to her own ears. Another shot buzzed in close by. Briggs was too exposed, and she didn't know what could be done about it. Whoever was shooting didn't seem to mind taking him out as well.

"Just hang on. We'll be back at the barn soon. It's the closest structure, and we need cover until we can get some backup here. See if you have cell service. Call the deputy and drop him a pin of our location."

Madison felt silly for not thinking of

that sooner and did as he asked. She sent the message just as a stray shot hit one of their tires, sending the UTV into a fishtail. Briggs fought to get the vehicle under control so it didn't flip, and Madison squealed and hung on tightly. The UTV whipped around before Briggs was finally able to get it stopped.

"Run!" he yelled, making a grab for her hand.

Madison stumbled out of the UTV and sprinted after him, Briggs tugging her along the whole time. They were in the open, at a serious disadvantage. The shooter was hiding out in the distant tree line. Dim light shone from the sliver of moon hiding in the cloudy sky, and the only clue that they had of the shooter's whereabouts was the distant hum of a motor from some type of smaller ATV coming from a distance. As long as their attacker was alone, he couldn't shoot and drive, so that at least gave them a little bit of hope.

There was no cover anywhere close, so they would have to sprint some distance before they could catch their breath. Madison had to force the fatigue back.

Just keep running. Don't think about it.

The air was insufficient to keep her going much longer, though. She ran for distance sometimes to keep fit, but never like this. The pace Briggs set was relentless. Her lungs stopped burning and went straight to a panicked freeze. It was excruciating. She knew she was slowing down, but she couldn't help it.

"Just a little farther," Briggs encouraged her. She didn't know how he could possibly find enough air to speak. She didn't answer.

He looked back, and without even breaking stride, he swooped her up and tossed her over his shoulder.

At that moment, another shot whizzed past. He jumped ahead, seeming to run even faster than before. Madison was in awe even as she struggled to take in air. Was this what SEAL training had taught him? How to be superhuman?

His wide shoulder bit into her midsection, and she braced for every jolt, but she was still thankful for his physical strength and endurance. No amount of adrenaline would have rescued her from this situation had she been alone.

At last, they reached the barn and ducked behind it. Briggs set her feet on the ground, opened the door, and ushered her inside. She stumbled into the barn in relief, still gasping and aching from lack of oxygen.

"How are you not suffocating right now? You're barely even breathing hard." Madison knew it was an odd thing to be thinking at such a time, but her thoughts sometimes just came out of her mouth.

He laughed. "How are you so worried about a little thing like breathing when your life is at stake? We probably don't have long. He'll try something else when he finds out he missed."

"Good point." Madison shrugged. "Are we safe in here?"

"For a little while, anyway. I don't know what happened to the deputy. He should have made it to us by now." Briggs pointed toward the tack room. "Take cover in there until I can see where the threat is. I'll check in with you in a few minutes."

Madison did as he asked and slid down the wall to sit on the cold concrete floor, the comforting scent of saddle leather surrounding her. She was beginning to catch her breath, but exhaustion was her worst enemy. She wanted to curl into a ball and never move again.

She could hear Briggs moving around the barn, opening the side doors and trying to draw fire to get the shooter to reveal his location. No shots were fired, though, and Madison felt uneasy in the silence. It was eerie and unsettling, like the calm before the tornado had struck.

It seemed ages ago at this point, but she couldn't help feeling the parallel deeply. She stood and opened the door, leaning out just a bit.

"Briggs," she called to him in a stage whisper.

He looked in her direction. "Stay put. Something's up."

Reassured that he felt it, too, she ducked back into the tack room. Waiting was torturous, though. She listened intently but could hear nothing at all. No doubt Briggs was watching and waiting to see what would happen.

Finally, he put his head in the tack room. "I tried calling the deputy again, but there's no answer. I don't know what's going on. I'm calling Dispatch to see if they can figure it out. Can you text your dad and have him send Lance and a couple of the guys out to get the UTV as soon as it's safe?"

She nodded, and he disappeared again. She tried her father's cell phone but got no answer. She sent him a text asking him to call her back. She was about to try again when her cell phone began to ring. It was Mrs. Newman calling from the house phone.

"Madison, it's your father. I think he's having a heart attack. I've called an ambulance, but he's asking for you." Mrs. Newman's voice wavered, cracking across the line in obvious fear.

"I'm on my way." Madison disconnected and threw open the door.

"Briggs! We have to get to the house. It's my dad. His heart." She blurted out the problem in spurts, but he seemed to understand.

"Let me go. You should stay here. It's safer." He tried to deter her with one hand.

"You can't expect me to stay here. Mrs. Newman said my father's asking for me. And who knows how bad it is."

He hesitated. "You're right. But I feel like something's up."

She squared up to him with her hands on her hips. "Of course I am. I'll have to take my chances with the gunshots. Besides, maybe if we both go, the shooter won't know who to shoot at."

He shook his head and made a noise of disbelief. "That's some convoluted logic. Maybe it just means they are more likely to hit someone."

She huffed. "Look, we could argue about it all day, but we need to go."

He nodded. "You're right. Let's go."

When they reached the door leading out of the barn, he looked back at her again. "Stay low and move fast."

She nodded, and they rushed across the yard. It was mere seconds before the gunfire began again. Some of the shots were close, sending Madison's adrenaline spiking up even higher. Briggs stayed near her, his presence a continuous reassurance despite their situation.

A sudden grunt from Briggs sent Madison into a new panic. "What's wrong?" Her gait hitched.

"Keep going. It grazed my side. I'll be fine." His voice sounded strained, but she did as he asked.

When they reached the back door at last, she stumbled in. Briggs slammed the door closed behind them just as another shot splintered the wood. Madison jumped and shrieked in response.

"In here!" Mrs. Newman called from the living room. "I gave him his medicine, but it isn't working."

Adria stood with Mrs. Newman, wringing her hands in uncertainty. Madison rushed in and knelt beside her father, who was stretched out on the sofa near the TV. She began speaking to him softly, noting his ashen gray pallor. His breathing was labored, sending waves of fear through her.

"Stay with me, Dad." She grasped his hand, and he nodded.

"Trying...my best." He was limp and clammy, and Madison didn't know what to do.

A shot shattered a window somewhere in the house, and Madison was reminded that the danger was twofold. Adria jumped and paled.

"Where is that deputy?" Briggs wondered aloud. "Something is off." He tapped at his cell phone again.

Madison didn't have time to worry about his actions, for her father sucked in a sharp breath. "Dad! Hang on." She rubbed his weathered hand.

Another shot fired, blasting the side of the house.

"Come on now. We aren't coming back

out. This guy is just being annoying," Briggs said, phone still to his ear. When someone from Dispatch finally picked up, he ducked out of the room.

The wait was excruciating, made worse by the intermittent gunshots. The women chattered nervously, all of them trying to think of something they could do to help Jake.

A moment later, when Briggs returned, he had told them the dispatcher was trying to reach the patrol deputy but wasn't getting through. He was awaiting a return call on the deputy's status.

Briggs had declared his injury to be just a scratch, quietly bandaging his wound with some ointment and gauze. After pacing for a few seconds, he disappeared again from the room to call the bunkhouse to let them know what was happening.

The shots stopped at last when the sirens became audible in the distance. The shooter must have assumed it was police backup and retreated.

Lights flashed in the window, and Madison breathed a sigh of relief as EMTs jumped from the ambulance. She met them at the door, giving them directions. "He's in here."

The EMTs went to work, loading her father onto a gurney and starting an IV. One asked about what treatment he had received so far, and Mrs. Newman handed them the medicine bottle.

"Strange that this isn't working. Mind if I take this with us?" The EMT looked puzzled as he stared at the label.

"Of course. Go ahead." Madison waved a hand toward the bottle.

The other EMT leaned over Jake on the gurney, giving them an urgent look. "We've gotta go. I think he's crashing."

ELEVEN

Briggs reentered the living room just in time to hear the EMT's declaration.

He grabbed Madison by the hand. "Come on. We'll follow them to the hospital." He was waiting for her to collapse, but she stood strong.

Adria followed them out, as did Mrs. Newman.

"I forgot my purse. I'll just take my car and follow." Adria gave them an apologetic look.

Mrs. Newman was already in the truck waiting for them, so Briggs nodded and urged Madison to hurry. It wasn't necessary, though.

When the ambulance pulled out with lights and sirens blaring, Briggs pulled out right behind them. "Dispatch still can't reach the deputy. They are sending someone else out to check on him. Lance and Stockton are out looking for his car. I assumed he was out patrolling the perimeter of the ranch, but no one has seen him."

He was trying to keep Madison's thoughts on something besides her dad. She was looking really pale and anxious, worry etching lines in her countenance. Careening after a speeding ambulance that held her sick father was stressful for him, so there was no telling how it was affecting her.

She turned away from the lights flashing in front of her. "I'm sorry for all this trouble. I know you have work to do on the ranch. You need to be getting your rest for tomorrow."

He laid a hand over hers where it rested on the console. A flare of awareness shot through him, but he did his best to keep his tone level. "Nothing is more important than keeping you safe and your father well."

Madison smiled slightly, probably the best she could. "I appreciate that more than you know."

They were both silent a moment, but Mrs. Newman cleared her throat from the back seat, reminding them of her presence. "Maybe we should let the hospital know what's going on ahead of time so they can amp up their security."

"That's a great idea. Did anyone happen to catch the name of the hospital the EMTs were headed for?" Briggs looked at the two women each in turn.

"I thought the woman said something about going to Grace Memorial," Mrs. Newman replied.

"I'll give them a call." Madison began to navigate on her phone, but her hands were trembling.

"Let me talk to them. Just find the number and dial it for me." Briggs held a hand out for the phone after she nodded.

He spoke briefly to the hospital receptionist, who then put him on with hospital security. He explained the situation and asked that they be prepared. They promised to call in some backup, including an extra patrol car from the local police force. He relayed the information to the ladies, mostly to reassure them and keep their thoughts occupied with something other than how Jake might be faring.

They hadn't made it far before a vehicle sped up on their bumper. "Oh, not this again," Briggs said.

Madison came alive. "I'm calling 911. This is getting out of hand."

"They are doing all they can. I'll try to lose them. Call Adria and tell her to take a different route if she can. I don't want her to get caught in the middle of this." Briggs was a little surprised by her sudden take-charge attitude. It seemed her would-be killer had pushed her too far.

She dialed and gave the dispatcher quite an assertive talk and then turned to Briggs. "They're sending someone out right away."

He just nodded, focused on his mission. "I'm trying to lose them but not having much success."

His words were punctuated by a shot pinging off the tailgate of the truck. Before he could warn them to get down, both women had hit the floorboard.

"Briggs, can I use your gun?" Madison held up her hand.

"What?" He was completely taken aback, but he kept his eyes on the dark, narrow road ahead.

"Maybe if I return fire, he will back off. I can shoot straight." Her expression was earnest.

He pulled the Glock out carefully, checking that the safety was on before handing it to her.

"I have had a bad night, and I am honestly tired of it. I'm more than ready to fight back?" She looked worse than irritated. She looked downright angry.

He swallowed back his reservations. It might help the situation. The car had backed off temporarily but was gaining on them again. "Okay. When they come close again, aim for the tires."

"Not the windshield? If I shatter the

glass, it could make it harder to see us to keep up." She clicked the safety off.

"That might not be a bad idea, actually. Easier target, too. Whatever will slow him down." Briggs glanced at his mirrors again.

Another shot hit the bumper, and Mrs. Newman uttered a mild exclamation from the back seat. "Someone should do something."

Madison leaned out the window, took aim, and returned fire. The windshield of the car following them crackled into a web of shattered glass. She announced her hit, and Mrs. Newman gave a cheer.

Briggs waited for her to lean back in the window and then punched the gas. He had lost the ambulance a ways back at an intersection, and he wondered if he should take another route to the hospital.

"Where is that backup we are supposed to be getting?" Briggs maneuvered around a pothole with a quick swerve.

"Ow!" Madison said as she slid into the door.

"Sorry. I need to concentrate." Briggs shrugged.

Their tail tried to come in close again, the driver occasionally poking his head out to get a better look. More shots came at regular intervals, but Madison fired back, and the other vehicle swerved and backed off again. Briggs was finally able to speed ahead a bit out of range. The headlights faded a little and then gained on them again.

Finally, police lights appeared in the distance, and the vehicle behind them braked and turned off on a side road. A patrol car followed, and another pulled over with Briggs.

He hopped out and spoke to the officer briefly, telling him what had happened with the car. They both eyed the bullet holes on the truck before Briggs spoke again. "We are trying to get to the hospital. They just took my ranch foreman in an ambulance."

"You'll get there quicker with an escort,"

the officer offered. "Let me just radio Dispatch, and we'll get you there right away."

Relief filled Madison as soon as they arrived at the ER and she was told her father was going to be okay, but the wait to see him with her own eyes was almost more than Madison could tolerate. Briggs informed her he needed to make a call as she went on in to see her father.

She gently hugged her dad, careful of the IV and monitors still connected to him in various places. "I was so scared for you."

"Oh, I'm too tough to let a little thing like a cantankerous ticker do me in." He offered her a weak smile.

"I'm thankful for that. I'm pretty sure your heart isn't the only thing cantankerous about you." She patted his hand. "Now to get you well and get you home."

They exchanged a few more words before Briggs and Mrs. Newman came in. While Mrs. Newman spoke to her father, Briggs drew her attention. "Can you step out into the hall with me for a moment?"

"Of course." She followed him out the door. "What is it?"

"A couple of things. First, they found Carl, the deputy that went missing. Officers found him out in the woods near a neighbor ranch, disoriented and unsure what happened. They suspect he was drugged somehow and dumped where he couldn't intervene." Briggs delivered the news stoically.

"That's awful," Madison exclaimed. "Will he be okay?"

"Yes, he'll be fine. But there is more bad news." His mouth was a hard line. "You remember the EMTs asked about your father's medicine?"

Madison nodded. "They thought it was odd that it didn't work."

"There's a very good reason it didn't work. Someone switched the actual medicine out with sugar pills." Briggs's face was red, and she knew he was as angry as she was, but it didn't ease the fury welling up in her.

"How? And who would do such a thing?"

Madison clenched her fists together. It was one thing to threaten her, but using her sick father as some sort of pawn infuriated her.

"I don't know, but we are going to find out." Briggs didn't say more, but she could tell there was much more on his mind.

"Do you think Adria is okay? I thought she would be here by now. I sent her a text, but she still hasn't answered." Madison looked at her phone screen again to be sure.

"She might have had to take a longer route. If she isn't here soon, try calling. Maybe she just can't get to her phone. It might be easier to answer a call over Bluetooth than to return a text." Briggs watched a doctor walk by and nodded a greeting.

Madison agreed. "I'll give her a few minutes longer. Right now, I want to know what's going on with Dad."

A nurse walked by then, giving them a questioning look. "Is everything okay?"

Madison nodded. "Can you tell us anything about when they will discharge Jake Burke?"

The nurse asked her identity and then nodded. "I'll check for you."

The nurse disappeared down the hall, and out of the corner of her eye, Madison saw a shadow moving beyond the nurse's station. She wouldn't have looked up if not for the concerned nurse. She quietly spoke Briggs's name to draw his attention and jerked her head in the direction of the shadow.

"Stay here." He strode toward the nurse's station, but before he reached it, a wiry man shot out from behind a cabinet.

The man turned to fire at Madison, but a laundry cart stood between them and Madison ducked behind it. When the gunman saw security as well as Briggs rushing toward him, he dropped the weapon to his side and slipped into the nearby stairwell. Briggs followed, as did the security officers, and Madison, hunkering behind the laundry cart, lost sight of them all as the door to the stairwell slammed shut.

When the men had all disappeared, Madison rose from her place of cover to hurry back to her father's room. Just then, a few feet to her left, an elevator door opened. Adria stood inside. She took one look at Madison and started asking questions.

"Madi? What's going on now? Is your dad okay? There are security officers everywhere, and the police are crawling all over the parking lot." Adria's eyes were wide, and she glanced around the hospital floor before departing the elevator.

Madison breathed a sigh of relief. "I'm so glad to see you're okay. I was getting worried, especially with everything that's happening. Dad is going to be okay. Someone switched his medicine for sugar pills."

"Oh, Madi, that's terrible. Who would do something like that?" Adria looked horrified. "I'm so glad he's going to be all right."

"That's not all." Madison gestured toward the stairwell. "Someone was lurking in the shadows watching us, and he pulled a gun on me. Briggs went after him. I don't know what's going on."

"No way! Even at the hospital? With

all this security?" Adria looked around. "What can I do? I know you need to be with your father. Is he alone?"

"Mrs. Newman is fussing over him at the moment." Madison smiled. "She's very good at that. Sweet woman. But, yes, I want to go check on Dad."

"She is something, isn't she? Definitely the motherly type." Adria smiled, too. "How about I wait here and you go check on your father?"

Madison walked in to see the tall, slim woman adjusting blankets around Jake as she chattered at him about something. She looked up when Madison walked in.

"He's being difficult, I must warn you." Mrs. Newman shook her head at him. "He thinks being in a little pain is grounds for acting like a two-year-old overdue for a nap."

"I am not acting like a two-year-old. I just want something besides weak tea or water to drink. I asked the nurse a long time ago." Jake huffed, settling back onto his pillow.

"It hasn't been five minutes," Mrs. Newman argued.

A few minutes passed in similar conversation, but Madison's anxiousness didn't ease. Now that she could see her father was recovering, she was concerned about the intruder and Briggs's safety.

"What are you not telling me, Madison?" her dad asked, obviously noticing her silence.

She hesitated only a second. "Someone bypassed security, and Briggs went after him. I need to know he's okay. I'll be back. I'm going to go check on him."

She slipped out the door and ran to the stairwell before any of them could protest. Looking down, she saw no sign of anyone, so she went to find the closest security officer and asked if he had any news.

He shrugged. "I don't know what you mean. I just got here."

Madison thanked him and took the elevator to the ground floor. She walked around until she saw a group of uniformed men gathered at a table outside the hospital coffee shop.

"Excuse me, but do any of you know where I can find Briggs Thorpe or learn what became of the man he chased in the stairwell?" Madison searched their faces as they turned her way.

A plump man with a distinctly country accent answered her. "Sorry, ma'am, but the man in the stairwell managed to escape. There was a fella running after him, but the city officers took over from there." According to their badges, these guys were hospital security. Their current attitudes might explain how the breach had occurred. She shook her head as the group went back to chatting and sipping coffee. How could they be so unconcerned?

She was about to thank them and go back up to her father's room when the main doors slid open, and Briggs walked in.

"Madison, why aren't you upstairs?" Briggs ran a hand over his brow.

She strode toward him. "I was worried about you. He got away?"

"Not exactly." He grinned. "Local police are taking him in for questioning. I had to fill them in on the latest. That's what took me so long."

"What?" She glanced back at the security officer who had said the gunman got away. "But they said—"

"I ran out a different door and cut him off. Security was too slow to keep up." A shrugged accompanied his words.

"Briggs Thorpe, were you a track star in your high school days?"

He shrugged. "I was too busy playing football."

Madison chuckled. "Well, I hope you played running back."

They hopped on the elevator and returned to Jake's room, where the nurses were finishing up paperwork for his release. When they came in, the nurse pulled Madison aside, and Briggs followed.

"You're his daughter?" The nurse clarified before speaking further.

"Yes, I am." Madison tilted her head.

"My name is Kayla. Dr. Franks said your

father should be fine as long as he keeps taking his meds. Just keep a close watch. I'm sure you know how serious his condition can be if he doesn't have the proper medication." The nurse searched her face.

Madison nodded. "I'm baffled over how the switch to sugar pills happened. No one had access to his medicine other than people we trust."

The nurse glanced around the room before leaning close. "Then maybe you'd better be careful who you trust."

TWELVE

Briggs didn't want to agree with the nurse, but he was beginning to wonder. Someone had to have replaced the pills, but who could it have been? There were people in and out of the house sometimes besides family, like the hands, but no one he mistrusted. Mrs. Newman was basically family, and Adria had nothing to gain by seeing her best friend's father get sick. It was baffling. Had it just been an effort to get them off the ranch? Anyone close to Madison had to know she would follow her father to the hospital.

The ride back to the ranch was uneventful. Once they had Jake settled again, he tried to get Madison to go and rest as well.

It was late, and she hadn't had any time to rest in the past couple of days.

"I don't think I can, honestly. I just want to watch a little TV or something until my mind settles down." Madison sat down on the couch and slipped off her shoes.

"Mind if I stay up with you for a little bit?" Briggs didn't want to be a nuisance if she wanted to be alone, but talking might help.

"I don't mind at all. I'd like to get your thoughts, anyway." She lifted an eyebrow at him. "If that's okay?"

Briggs sat down beside her with a sigh. "Yeah, but I really don't know what to think. It's so odd that this all started in Boston and has only gotten worse here. They found the deputy's car out along the south pasture. He apparently tried to radio in, but someone cut the connection. I asked to speak to the deputy, but he doesn't remember anything. And why is the perp desperate enough to try to harm your father? It makes sense that they would come after me since I've been protecting you the best I can, but why hurt your father?"

"Do you think it has to do with vengeance?" Madison squinted blankly at the wall. "The only other reason to do it would be to draw us out, but how could they know when the medicine would stop working? It doesn't seem like that would be an effective way to do it."

Briggs shook his head. "No, that wouldn't make sense, for sure. Maybe they planned it hoping it would keep you closer to the house."

"Why, though? What purpose could they have for wanting me here and not out working the ranch? Wouldn't I be an easier target out there somewhere?" Madison tucked one foot beneath her.

"It seems you would, yes." He sat back against the cushions, trying for a moment to think like an assassin.

Mrs. Newman appeared at the door. "Adria asked me to let you know that she's retired for the evening. I'm about to do the same. If you need anything or if Jake gets worse in the night, please wake me."

Briggs nodded, and Madison watched as Mrs. Newman departed.

"What?" Briggs prodded. "You're thinking something."

"Mrs. Newman is a widow, is she not?" Madison couldn't keep the grin from teasing the corners of her mouth.

"Yes, for several years, like your father. What are you— Oh, no. Don't start matchmaking." Briggs shook his head.

Madison laughed. "I don't think I have to. She seems awfully concerned about him. Very attentive. And he doesn't seem to mind."

Briggs considered that for a moment. "Now that you say that, they have been pretty close lately."

"That's good. I was beginning to wonder if this place was for singles only. Everyone here seems to be suffering from being alone."

"I wouldn't say anyone is suffering, ex-

actly. Some of us choose to be single."
Briggs frowned.

Madison tilted her head at him. "Oh?
Does that include you?"

"I haven't had much success with romance. I don't even date anymore." Briggs
hoped she would drop it. He really didn't
want to talk about it.

"I haven't, either. I don't really know
how people ever make it work. It's so difficult to find someone like-minded and
trustworthy."

"I have to agree there. What happened to
make you feel that way?" Briggs knew he
shouldn't ask when he didn't want to tell
his own story, but he couldn't stop himself.

"I dated Jonas for about three years. I
fell in love with him as soon as we met.
He treated me like a princess. I thought I
knew everything there was to know about
him. He proposed on Christmas Eve with
all of his family present, and it was all
so surreal. I thought he was as happy as
I was, but a few weeks before the wedding, he confessed he had been secretly

seeing someone else. It turned out to be his old high school sweetheart. They had remained friends over the years, and it seems he never really got over her. He broke off the wedding, and I never heard from him again. I was completely blindsided."

"Yikes. No wonder you don't want to date." Briggs waited. She would want to know his story now.

She surprised him by rising from the sofa instead. "I could really use some water. Would you like anything?"

Briggs shook his head and watched her go. He couldn't imagine anyone finding someone to replace a woman like Madison. She was everything good and beautiful, and he had no idea how anyone could be better.

She had been so strong through all of this. He wanted nothing more than to figure out who was behind this and give her some peace. She deserved it, and he was beginning to feel like a failure because he hadn't figured it out yet.

When Madison returned, she settled

back on the sofa and asked him about the ranch. "You haven't had a chance to visit Miranda since I got here. Would you mind taking me soon?"

"Absolutely. I would love to take you, but tomorrow we have to get the buffalo rounded back up. The heifers need to be checked. We have a lot to do, and we should probably wait until this is over before we drag danger to her door."

Madison nodded. "You're right. I almost forget sometimes, but I understand. You don't know how much I miss Wade when I'm here."

The comment caught him off guard. "You were really close, huh?"

Madison smiled. "Like brother and sister. We fought like siblings sometimes, too."

"But never anything romantic?" He raised an eyebrow at her.

"No. I guess we thought about it for a split second in high school, but we kissed and were both immediately convinced it wasn't where we were headed." Madison laughed. "There was just no spark."

"Ah. Everyone wants the spark, huh?" Briggs looked at her for a moment with a twinkle in his eye.

Madison sobered. "I thought I had that with Jonas. I guess he felt otherwise."

Briggs frowned then. "Well, he was a fool."

Wishing he hadn't said it, Briggs turned away. Madison was silent, probably wondering where such a proclamation had come from. He rose, desperate to put some space between them.

"We'd better try to get some rest. Tomorrow has its own worries."

Madison nodded and rose to leave as well. "Yes, you're right. Good night."

"Good night, Madison." He followed her down the hall to the rooms, making sure she was safely inside her own. Then he went into his and threw back the covers. He settled in and sighed in appreciation, but he soon found there was far too much on his mind to sleep.

* * *

Madison woke early the next morning, surprised she had been able to get a good night's rest at last. She dressed to go and help with the bison but found the kitchen empty when she came down. She poured a cup of coffee and sat down at the kitchen table with it.

Mrs. Newman appeared in the doorway. "Good morning. Would you like some eggs and toast? Or pancakes, maybe?"

Madison smiled. "Good morning. Just toast would be fine."

Mrs. Newman nodded. "You look rested. Finally got a peaceful night?"

Madison was sipping her coffee and paused. "It was nice, but I'm afraid it won't last. Where is Briggs? I thought he'd be up and ready to go."

"Oh, he's been here and already gone. One of the hands said he had a heifer having trouble calving, so Briggs took off." Mrs. Newman gestured out the window.

Madison glanced outside. "I wonder if he needs help."

The look on Mrs. Newman's face held a knowing quality, like she was privy to a secret. "I'm sure it wouldn't hurt. I can see to your father if he wakes before you return."

"Hold off on that toast." Madison rose, leaving her mostly full cup of coffee. "I'm going to go see if I can help."

"Suit yourself." Mrs. Newman chuckled. "At least take that coffee to go." She poured it into a mug with a lid and handed it to Madison, who then slipped out the back door.

The morning was cloudy, and it looked like another storm could brew up any time. No wonder the heifer had chosen now to calve. It seemed the silly animals always gave birth in the worst weather possible.

She saddled Kat quickly, keeping the mare's grooming brief, and took off in the direction they had gone to check the heifers a couple of days before. She kept watch over her shoulder and all around, but the ranch was strangely quiet and peaceful.

When she saw Briggs at last, he was bent

down with the heifer, examining her carefully. Stockton stood behind him. They both looked up when they heard Madison's horse approaching.

"You're up early." Briggs sounded a little curt.

Madison ignored his sharp tone. "Looks like she's having a tough go of it. Can I help?"

Briggs sat back. "Actually…you could. Calf is breech. You have smaller hands. Maybe you can turn it."

Madison's eyes widened. "You want me to turn the calf?"

He nodded, and Stockton chuckled. "Unless you're too squeamish."

She laughed. "Not at all. I'm just surprised you would trust me to do such a thing. I've never turned a breech calf before."

"That's okay. I will guide you through it." Briggs's tone had softened. "If you're sure you don't mind, we need to start now. She's been struggling a while and is losing strength."

Madison nodded. Stockton reached into the UTV and handed her some long gloves. They were too big on her, and she hesitated for a moment before stripping them back off.

"I think I'll fare better without them." She disinfected her hands and arms as best she could with sanitizing agents, but there was no time to go back to the barn to scrub. The mother and calf stood more risk of dying from an inability to get the calf through the birth canal than from a secondary infection. They would just have to give her antibiotics and keep her under a veterinarian's care afterward.

The men nodded and grinned as Madison pushed her sleeves up onto her shoulders.

At Briggs instruction, she reached in and began to push the calf back up into the birth canal. The heifer began to bawl in protest, but Stockton held the mother-to-be's head and spoke to her, calming her down.

"Once the calf is back far enough, see

if you can find its front feet. They should be at the opposite end of where you just pushed." Briggs continued to give her calm, clear instructions, and soon she had the calf by the front feet.

It was a tedious process, one that she feared was taking too long for the heifer's well-being. But she didn't want to cause more damage than good, so she took her time and finally had the calf positioned front feet first, as it was supposed to be.

Briggs spoke encouragingly to her as she began to pull. Stockton implored the heifer to push, but she was weak and not making much effort. Briggs kept both hands on the heifer's abdomen, and when he felt a contraction moving through her, he told Madison to pull.

She gripped the slippery legs as tightly as she could, sat back on her heels, and tugged with all her might.

"That's it! The calf is coming. Good girl, Mama." Briggs stroked the cow as she panted, eyes wide.

The tiny hooves were out. Madison kept

pulling, and a little pink nose appeared. Briggs reached in and cleared his tiny nostrils. She kept up the steady pressure as the shoulders, probably the widest part of the calf, began to slip out. Once they cleared, the rest of the calf easily progressed. As the calf's buttocks hit the ground, Madison sighed in relief, releasing the slippery little legs.

"You did it. Way to go!" Briggs was grinning widely at her. The mama cow let out a long cry of relief.

Madison looked at the tiny wet calf just beginning to stir around on the ground. The heifer shifted and began to lick her baby. Madison felt a surge of appreciation for God's wonderful creation. She uttered a silent prayer of thanks.

"Nice job!" Stockton clapped her on the shoulder. "Looks like they are both gonna be fine, thanks to you."

"I'm sure you guys would have managed." But satisfaction poured through her at the idea that she had done some good for this pair of animals. She was thankful she had succeeded, and especially glad for Briggs guiding her through it. She might have figured it out, but not without having to tackle her doubts and nerves.

They stayed with the cow and calf for a little while until the calf finally stood and began nursing from the mother.

"I think they're going to be fine." Briggs motioned that they should leave. "We'd better get that herd gathered up and put in the right pasture."

Madison noticed how weary he looked. "When do you rest?"

Briggs shook his head. "There's no time for rest right now. I rest when things are taken care of. It evens out eventually."

Madison couldn't help thinking that would be rough. "Well, I'm helping. Mrs. Newman has Dad's care under control, and I'm at your disposal. We need to beat the storm this time."

She glanced at the dark morning sky. The sun had been up for over an hour, but clouds kept it from shining. She frowned.

The last thing they needed was a repeat of the last fiasco.

"We'll take the UTV back and get the hands gathered up. You'd better ride along." Briggs pressed his lips together.

Madison simply nodded, and when the men had loaded into the side-by-side, she trailed them on Kat.

The other hands were already saddling horses when they returned. Madison watered Kat and loosened the mare's girth while she went to clean up from helping deliver the calf. She came back with a treat for Kat while they waited. The mare was going to have a busy morning. Before long, everyone was gathered up, and Briggs gave them the plan.

Much to Madison's relief, they had the herd rounded back up in a short amount of time with no complications. Some of the bison even wandered through the open gate and settled into the new pasture on their own.

Fatigue weighed on them all, so they shut the bison into the pen and dispersed to the house without ceremony. Madison was glad to get back to check on her father. She found Mrs. Newman reading to him from the New Living translation of the Bible, and she ducked out shortly after making sure he was okay. Adria was sitting alone in the living room, so she joined her there.

Briggs didn't waste any time getting back to the work that still needed to be done, leaving the women to visit.

"What is there to do around here besides ride horses and work cows?" Adria joked.

Madison teased her back. "Oh, you know. You can go fishing and catch lightning bugs after dark, but we have a few hours before that."

"Oh, sounds like a good ole time." Adria laughed.

"I could show you around the ranch if you like. You don't have to ride. Briggs has a UTV that is used for work. He might be willing to let me use it to give you a tour."

"I don't want to inconvenience Briggs. He seems to be pretty busy." Adria shook her head. "Maybe I'll go to the city. I need to do some shopping, anyway. Do you want to go?"

Madison shook her head. "I don't think that's a good idea right now. I know you aren't really that interested in the ranch, but I really can't take the chance on leaving right now. It's too dangerous."

"You're right. I'm not thinking clearly," Adria agreed. "The ranch is cool, but I do feel pretty out of my element here."

"Maybe it would be a good idea for you to return to Boston. I don't want you to get hurt." Madison looked out the window. More clouds were gathering, and the spring wind was gusting through the trees with a fury. "The weather seems to be turning bad again, anyway."

Adria pressed her lips together for a moment. Frau had curled up on her lap, and she stroked him absently. "I know you're probably right, but I just can't leave you right now. I need to know you're safe."

Mitzi started to bark then, pulling their attention away from the window.

"What is it, girl?" Madison stood and strode to the door behind the Pomeranian.

Mitzi continued to bark and growl. Looking out the sidelights beside the door carefully, Madison kept her body to one side. "I don't see anything. Maybe just a squirrel or the wind blowing leaves around."

"Silly pup." Adria laughed. "Maybe she needs to go out to take care of business?"

"It has been a while, but she doesn't usually act like this when she needs to go out. Maybe she just wants to go out and play," Madison said.

"I'll take her out," Adria offered, starting to push Frau aside.

"No, no. You two stay put. I'll take her out. It's no big deal. Briggs is only a few feet away in the barn, anyway." Madison opened the door and followed Mitzi out.

A squirrel shot past at that moment. The tiny dog darted across the yard, running as fast as her short legs could carry her.

"Mitzi, stop!" Madison yelled.

She closed the door behind her to go after the dog, calling for her to stop the whole time. Mitzi ignored her, heading out through the trees away from the house and barn. Madison followed, but every time she would get almost close enough to swoop up the little dog, Mitzi would take off again.

Madison was concentrating so hard on grabbing the Pomeranian before she got picked off by a hawk that she almost didn't notice the shadow that fell across her path. When she looked up, a man in a black ski mask held a gun pointed right at her.

THIRTEEN

Briggs saw Madison dart across the yard after Mitzi as he led a horse out to the round pen. He dismissed it at first, since he saw her little dog zoom ahead of her. However, when several minutes passed and she didn't reappear, he grew concerned.

Handing off the young filly he was working with to Stockton, he made his way across the yard in the direction he had last seen her. He saw no sign of her and began to trek through the shadows under the stand of sycamores and oaks. Madison must have gone farther into the trees than he expected.

His worry intensified when he saw Mitzi, or rather he heard her. She had her bushy fur snagged in a blackberry bramble and couldn't seem to free herself.

He knelt and cut her lose with the small Case knife he carried in his jeans pocket, not concerned about the scruffy haircut the Pom was now sporting. "Where's your mom, little girl?"

Mitzi licked him gratefully with her petite pink tongue but continued to whine. "I know she wouldn't have left you."

The pup was a little wet underneath her belly and had some stickers from the blackberry bush stuck in her fur. Briggs picked the dog up and stroked her fur. Mitzi settled down, and he focused on finding Madison.

Searching the muddy ground for clues, he made his way slowly through the trees, hoping to see a sign of her somewhere. He could tell where she had walked into the trees on the wet ground, but leaves and rocks covered too much of the dirt to make a perfect trail. He wanted to see something a little more tangible pointing to her direction. He scanned the pebbly dirt. Nothing.

He was growing frustrated. She couldn't have gotten far, could she? Briggs covered every inch of ground he could under the trees until he finally saw an area of the damp dirt and leaves that looked disturbed. He strode over for a closer inspection and saw footprints, two sets. It looked like one was following closely behind the other. Too closely.

There was only one thing he could think of that might cause footprints like that. The next thought that entered his mind filled him with more terror than he had felt since Emily had gone missing.

Someone had forced Madison away under coercion. Her captor could have a gun to her head at this very moment.

Madison was overcome with cold fear. Was this it? Was her life about to be over before it had really begun? She thought of all the things she hadn't been able to experience—marriage, family, time spent with those she loved—so many things she had put on the back burner for her career and because of Jonas's betrayal. She saw now it didn't really matter.

Holding the gun to her head, her captor had forced her to walk out of the woods in the opposite direction from the house. She wasn't sure how he had known she would come out with her dog. Maybe he had just been lying in wait, thinking she would have to leave the house eventually. She felt it must have more to do with bad timing than a solid plan.

He made her walk all the way across the wooded edge of the property with the gun to her temple. She was shaking from sheer terror, and she worried the gun could go off at any time. As they walked closer to the road, a dark truck with tinted windows came into view, and she knew he at least intended to take her somewhere else before killing her. She puzzled over why, but she was grateful for the fact. It gave her a little more time. She was also determined to find a way to keep him from getting her in that truck.

She used all her mental energy to try to figure something out. She assumed he would either make her get in first while he held the gun on her or make her drive. So she would have to find a way to distract him before he could get her into the vehicle.

She tried to think of things she had heard of that had worked for others trying to escape an abductor, but nothing came to mind. The only thing she could think to do was talk.

"Why are you doing this?" She tried to keep her voice calm and even. "Have I done something to you? Help me understand. What did I do that caused this?"

He grunted. "Just doing what I'm told, lady."

"But why? And by whom? Did someone pay you to kidnap me? I'm certainly not worth any money." She wanted to make him see she was just a person. Maybe he would have second thoughts.

"Oh, I'm getting paid, all right. But only if I deliver you to the address they gave me. Get in the truck." He didn't move the gun from her temple or loosen his grip on her at all.

"You do realize my friends will come looking for me at any moment?" She tried another tactic.

It was apparently the wrong one. "Yeah, so hurry up."

She opened the door and edged closer to the truck. An idea occurred to her. It was risky, but she had to try. As she began to slide into the truck, she intentionally slipped, causing him to lose his grip on her as she fell. She would have a pretty good bump on her head, but it gave her a split second to react.

She grabbed the door handle and yanked the door into him, throwing him off balance. As he stumbled, she kicked out at him while the gun was loosely pointed at the ground. It fired harmlessly into the dirt beside the road while her captor tried to right himself. He muttered an expletive as he struggled to get back to his feet.

Madison was already running, though. She kicked the gun farther from him as she passed, anything to slow him down a little more.

He was on his feet and after her in no time, though, which she confirmed by looking over her shoulder. She pumped her legs as hard as she could, but he reached her too soon. He was breathing down her neck when she heard a wonderful sound.

"Stop or I'll shoot!"

It was Briggs's voice.

The man didn't stop, and she felt his hand brush against her shoulder just before a shot rang out. There was a howl of pain just behind her, and the sound of the man crumpling against the ground.

Madison slowed, putting her hands to her knees to catch her breath as soon as she saw the man lying helpless on the ground, a gunshot wound marring his upper thigh. His weapon was on the ground several feet away from him and Madison reached for it just in case.

Briggs bound the man with some twine left over in his pocket from putting out hay earlier and called the police. He took the ski mask from the man's face to see if they could identify him, and then stuck it in the man's mouth to stem the flow of expletives and moaning.

Madison handed Briggs the man's handgun once he was done. "I'm so happy to see you."

He gestured toward the man and the bruises beginning to form on his face. "It looks like you were doing a pretty good job of fighting back."

"I hit him with the truck door." She said it as if it was no big deal.

"I saw that." Briggs chuckled. "That was a bit risky, don't you think?"

Madison put a hand on her hip. "It worked, didn't it?"

"Didn't you think I'd come after you?" Briggs tilted his head to the side.

"I didn't think you would know where I had gone." She shrugged.

"I'm never too far away in case you need me. I try to keep watch. Sorry I didn't get here sooner." Briggs was staring intently at her.

Mitzi came running up then, barking viciously at the man tied on the ground.

"Where did she come from? I lost her."
Madison scooped the little dog up into her
arms.

"I found her and cut her loose from a
blackberry bush, but I had to put her down
to come after you. I guess she followed
me." Briggs looked back at the man still
writhing on the ground.

"Mitzi." Madison gently shook the Pom.
"You're a troublemaker."

The little dog continued to growl at the
man, paying Madison very little mind.
Madison looked at the man and shivered.
"He said someone hired him. I couldn't get
any more information out of him, though."

Briggs didn't appear to be too surprised
by that fact. "Are you okay?"

She wrapped her arms around herself.
"Yes. But I do wish we could find whoever
is behind this. I'm ready for it to be over."

"I understand that. We are doing everything we can. I was about to check in with
Avery, anyway. I'll do that as soon as we
get this man in custody."

Once the police came and took the man

into custody, they went back to the house. Briggs called his brother, but Avery told him he would have to call him back.

Madison watched Briggs as he paced along the porch, thoughts of the man himself filling her mind. She tried to wave the thoughts away. She had quickly developed feelings for him, and while she had worked very hard for her career, she found the thought of leaving him behind to go back to Boston caused a huge ache to begin in her chest.

And there was also her father. She hoped he had many good years left, but she already had the regret of not being here at the end of her mother's life. She didn't want to add to that by missing her father's remaining years.

It was too much to think about right now, considering someone was trying to kill her. She knew they were probably no closer to finding the culprit than they had been when she arrived, and she sincerely wanted it to all just go away. If only it were that simple.

But until it was resolved, she was thankful to have Briggs watching out for her. He made her feel safe. Well, at least as safe as anyone could feel with a murderer on their trail.

Looking around the ranch now, her view from the porch just compounded her dilemma. The beauty surrounding her filled her with wonder and a sense of coming home. She wrestled it back, not wanting to give in to it. She needed to accept that this wasn't the life intended for her anymore. She had made her choices, and they hadn't led her to this life. She could only live the life she had, but she would definitely need to come back and visit more often.

Still, it would be hard to come back and see Briggs and start missing him all over again. If he stayed here, she knew he would inevitably end up getting married... starting a family...living a life she couldn't give him.

Briggs sighed, making her curious about what was on his mind, but she didn't dare ask. It was safer to keep her distance. Even if, secretly, she wanted to know everything about him.

FOURTEEN

When Avery finally called back, Briggs paced the porch a few more minutes before slipping down the steps to the yard. He didn't say a lot when he returned, though. He really didn't have a great deal to tell her.

"My brother thinks he is getting close to finding something. He's actually on his way here."

"Where does your brother live?" Madison was looking off into the yard, but she finally turned and looked at him when she asked the question.

"Avery lives in Wyoming. So does my twin brother, Beau. Beau was headed to the Oklahoma City area to attend a large cattle sale, and Avery agreed to come with him." He answered absently, forgetting Madison didn't know his brothers.

Adria had slipped out onto the porch while he was speaking. "You have a twin brother?"

"Yes, I have four brothers. Beau is oldest by a few minutes. Then there is Grayson, Avery, and Caldwell is the youngest." Briggs didn't mind talking about his brothers. They were all pretty close. At least, they had been until recently, when Caldwell had distanced himself from the others.

"Wow. Big family, huh?" Adria moved to the edge of the porch to lean against a pillar.

"We wanted a sister. Never got one." He chuckled. "I'm not sure why. To make us a little less rough around the edges."

"What about your mother? How did she feel about being the only female in the house?"

"Not great, I guess. She left when we were all pretty young." Briggs frowned.

Before Adria could express the sympathy

that filled her face, the sound of gunshots began, sending them running for cover.

Adria shrieked, and Madison stumbled over to grasp her arm and help her into the house and out of harm's way.

"Where are those deputies?" Briggs didn't know how Madison's attacker kept getting by them.

The shots rang closer. He saw Madison practically shove Adria into the house, Madison shouting a warning to her father and Mrs. Newman. Briggs followed after a second.

"Stay inside and give me some cover. I'm going after him." Briggs told her where to find the rifle in the gun safe inside the house. "Your father knows the combination. I'll give you a minute to get the gun loaded. Be sure and stay low."

Madison nodded. "Adria can call the bunkhouse and see if any cowhands are close."

When Madison handed Adria the phone, she nodded.

Jake gave Madison the rifle and took out

a shotgun for himself. "I can still shoot," he assured them.

Madison and Jake took up positions at the front windows, knocking out the screens to get the gun barrels out. Once they were ready, Briggs ducked low and took off after the gunman.

Madison impressed him. She took aim and began to fire, keeping the gunman off guard until Briggs could get close. Her father pulled his own trigger and reloaded just an echo behind Madison. They fired a couple more times, but when Briggs got closer to the gunman, they lowered their weapons.

A figure in black took off running, and Briggs chased him. As he gained on the figure, he stumbled over a fallen tree limb, momentarily losing his balance. He surged ahead again after a few seconds, though, and managed to get close enough to knock the long-range rifle from the gunman. When the man tried to make a grab for it, Briggs tackled him.

The man missed the gun but pulled a

knife from his belt. Briggs was ready for it, though. He grasped the man's fore-arm and wrenched it roughly, striking his knife hand hard against the ground. The force made the man release his grip on the weapon. They began to struggle fiercely, but the man wasn't strong enough to over-power Briggs.

Suddenly, a pistol shot came from the di-rection of the road just as Briggs seemed to have him secured. It missed, but Briggs flinched, giving the man a second to slip loose. When Briggs tried to follow again, a shot kicked up dirt beside his feet. He couldn't see the second gunman, but he heard his shouts to stay where he was, so Briggs did, putting his hands up.

"Go get the girl," the second man said, stepping just clear of the woods. He wore camouflage clothing. Briggs first thought the order was for him, until the guy in camo glanced away from him.

His partner whined. "How am I sup-posed to do that alone?"

With an irritated expression, the man

holding the gun on Briggs seemed to lose his focus for a split second as his level aim slid down and his eyes shifted.

As the pistol lowered, a rifle shot pierced the air and bark splinters flew from the tree trunk near the whining man.

"Who was that?" the man in camo asked.

Another shot, this time close to the man with the pistol. It fell from his grasp.

Expletives colored the air. "Let's get out of here."

The black-clad gunman sprinted away to the edge of the trees. He shouted something unintelligible and the man in camo followed. A road was on the other side, and there must have been a vehicle waiting for the gunmen there, because while Briggs was still standing with his hands in the air, he heard an engine roar to life and speed away.

Shots followed them. Briggs ducked, trying to discover their source. He dropped low and began to move toward them. A shout finally cleared up his confusion.

Madison. She was out here shooting back at the men.

He wasn't sure whether he wanted to throttle her or hug her.

He answered her inquiry about his welfare before sprinting back to the edge of the woods. He paused when he realized they didn't have any other backup. Where were the deputies?

He pulled out his cell phone to call 911. The dispatcher took down his information, and when Briggs asked about the deputies, the dispatcher told him they had been forced to bring in every available officer for a hostage situation in town. Briggs didn't think that was a coincidence at all. Especially since they informed him it had been a false alarm and the officers should be returning soon. At least, he hoped, the current threat was gone for now.

But when he got to the edge of the woods, he found both Madison and Mrs. Newman crouched behind the old ranch work truck with rifles in their hands.

"How…?" Briggs started to ask questions, but finally settled for gratitude. "Thank you."

"You didn't think we would just leave you to the wolves, did you?" Madison tossed him a wink. "I'm glad you're okay."

Madison didn't want to admit how scared she had been for Briggs's life only seconds before.

This had to end. Someone was going to get hurt, and she couldn't live with it. Adria could have been hit today. Briggs had also been in the line of fire many times while trying to protect her. She had to figure out who was doing this.

When she said so, Briggs grunted at her from his place on the steps. "You don't think we're trying?"

"I know you are. I guess I'm just angry at myself for not being able to figure this out. I'm sorry. What did you learn about the deputies?" Madison wrung her hands together. She was putting far too many people in danger, and she wanted it to stop.

"They were called out to an emergency by the dispatcher. It turned out to be a false alarm, but by the time it was canceled, the deputies were already en route. I'm sure the call was somehow connected to your attacker. They can't prove anything, though."

Madison plopped down on the steps. She couldn't help herself. There had to be something she was missing. "So tell me again what Avery said."

"I've told you three times already, Madison. You're going to make yourself ill. Just stop worrying for a little bit. I'm going to find your attacker." Briggs ran a hand through his dark hair, making it stand out in waves.

"How? I need a plan. We need to make this stop. Maybe if I hear the details again, it will trigger a realization." Madison crossed her arms over her chest.

"Madison…" He sat down beside her on the steps.

"I'm scared." She felt tears welling in her eyes and tried to blink them away.

Briggs pulled her into his arms. "I know you are, but we have to keep a cool head about this. Doing something rash might get someone killed. Just try to stay calm."

He stroked her back, and she realized how good his tender touch felt. It had been so long since a man had shown her tenderness. She had missed it more than she thought. It lulled her into a calmness, but somehow also made her a little reckless.

"Tell me why you aren't married." Her words were out before she had time to think, startling even her. She thought he would stiffen and refuse to answer, but he didn't.

"I was almost married once, actually." He kept stroking her back.

"When you were in the military?" She'd had no idea.

"No." He slowed his hand. "I had a high school sweetheart. We planned to get married. She went to college when I enlisted in the navy."

"You couldn't make a long-distance relationship work?" Madison leaned into his chest a little closer. She felt safe. Protected.

"Oh, we did. For a while. She graduated, and we made wedding plans. She was going to join me, and we were going to make a life together." He stopped stroking. "But she was killed before we could make that happen."

Madison raised her head in shock. "Killed? How?"

"Someone tried to abduct her, but she fought back hard, and the investigators think that they killed her because she was too much trouble. The evidence showed she did quite a bit of damage to her attacker before he—" Briggs cut himself off, his throat sounding tight. "Investigators thought it was probably associated with a human trafficking ring. They could never prove it, though. I wanted justice, but her killer was never found. That's when I joined the SEALs. I wanted to do everything I could to erase that kind of evil from the world, even if I never found her killer."

"Wow." Madison uttered the word quietly. "That's awful. What was her name?"

Briggs was silent for a moment, and she began to think he wouldn't answer, but at last, he did. "Her name was Emily. She was good in every sense of the word."

"I'm sure she was beautiful, inside and out. So that prompted you to join the SEAL team? But then you ended up injured and discharged?" Madison wanted to know everything. He was finally talking, and she didn't want it to stop. What made this man who he was? She wanted to know him better.

"Yeah. After that, I realized I was damaged goods, mentally and physically. I healed physically, but mentally... Well, I didn't want to subject any other woman to my issues from the past. So I don't even date."

She shook her head at him. "That's silly. A woman who loves you would understand. A woman who loves you would help you heal."

He looked into her eyes then. "I'm starting to see that."

She was suddenly all too aware of their closeness, her own breathing, and the rise and fall of his chest as his own breath hitched. His eyes were so blue, so caring and deep.

His gaze dropped to her lips then, and she leaned toward him. She knew she was taking a risk at losing her heart, especially with what he had just told her, but she needed his comfort. She wanted to feel his lips on hers, if only for this one moment.

When his lips touched hers, the tenderness she had previously felt dimmed in comparison. His kiss felt like coming home, like something inside her clicked into place.

It scared her witless.

She pulled back, afraid of what she would see in his eyes when she looked at him. It was a reflection of her own feelings, really. Sweet emotion mixed with uncertainty and fear. He wanted to comfort her as much as she wanted to draw comfort from his arms. And there was more. He had taken a huge step just by kissing her. She could see that. It meant more to him than she could fathom. She wanted to help him heal, and yet…she still had some healing to do of her own.

FIFTEEN

"Madison, I need to be honest with you," Briggs said as he settled at the kitchen table alone with her the next morning. "I am not ready for a relationship. I didn't mean to lead you on in any way last night."

She gave him a look he couldn't interpret. "I'm not either, Briggs. Maybe never again. No worries."

He opened his mouth to keep talking, but her expression silenced him. She looked hurt, despite her words. He didn't know how to approach that. Did she regret their tender moment as much as he did?

No, that wasn't entirely true. He didn't regret it. He only regretted that there couldn't be more of them. A lifetime of them, even. But he couldn't do that to her.

He couldn't attempt a relationship when he had no idea how that would work out with his emotional state being what it was. He didn't even know how to define it. He had heard of people having walls up, but he had an impenetrable fortress, and he wasn't even sure the heart behind it was still beating.

They ate their breakfast in silence until Adria came in.

"I will be leaving tomorrow. Madison, are you sure you don't want to come back with me? You could hire a bodyguard in Boston." Adria settled in a chair beside her with a cup of coffee and a blueberry muffin.

Madison looked at Briggs. "That seems a little risky. I'd better wait a few more days and see if we can't catch this guy."

Adria gave her a pouty look but patted her hand. "I understand. I just hate to go back without you. I was really hoping this would all be over by now."

"Me too." Madison scrunched up her face. "Maybe soon."

No more was said, but Briggs soon got up from the table. "I've got a lot to do. Madison, why don't you stay here and visit with Adria today? I think you'll be safe enough with everyone here and the deputies guarding the house. They'll be more cautious after what happened to Carl." He was referring to the deputy that went missing the night Jake had to be taken to the hospital.

"I'm sure they will." Madison shook her head. "That was awful."

"I'm just glad he is okay." Briggs poured his coffee into an insulated mug to take with him.

The women uttered their agreement, and Briggs excused himself. He had to get the equipment ready for hay baling season, and it didn't seem like something that Madison would want to help with. At least that was the excuse he gave himself. Truthfully, he needed time to think. He needed some time without her beside him to sort through the facts.

The day was sunny and cool. Wind blew

steadily, and Briggs was glad for the brisk breeze to help him clear his head. The baler hadn't been working properly when he finished hay season last year, so he needed to get it working correctly before the grass began to get tall.

He hoped having something else to focus his thoughts and energy on would help him keep his mind off Madison. Yes, he still needed to figure out who was targeting her, but it was the other thoughts that were driving him mad. The tender thoughts, the visions of a future with her here, living on the ranch with him for the rest of their days. Those were the thoughts he needed to extinguish. It was only a dream, a fairy tale. He couldn't take that risk again.

"You're sure deep in thought. Why so quiet today?" Lance asked the question as he stuck his head around one of the giant rubber belts hanging from the inside of the baler.

"I'm not quiet. Just thinking about how best to fix this. Might be time to think about replacing this old thing." Briggs patted the side of the hull, sending dust flying from the faded green paint.

Lance chuckled. "Situation's worse than I thought. I've never known you to give up on equipment with life left in it. Are you even thinking about the equipment, or are you thinking about Jake's daughter?"

Briggs shot him a look that made Lance throw his hands up in surrender.

"Sorry! I guess I shouldn't have asked. It just sure seems like there's a bit of something there, if you know what I mean. A fella could certainly do worse." Lance grinned.

"I'm not looking for a wife. Or even a girlfriend, for that matter." Why had he said that? Briggs swallowed hard. Surprise registered on Lance's face at the word *wife*. That had been the wrong thing to say.

"Okay, I get it. But sometimes God sends good things to us when we aren't really looking." Lance ducked his head into the baler and went back to work.

Briggs's mind kept replaying those last

words. *Sometimes God sends good things to us when we aren't really looking.*

Madison was restless.

She spent some time with her father, who wanted nothing more than to get outside. She took him to the porch for a few minutes, but the cool air was too much for him, and he soon wanted to go back inside. She sat talking with him for a little bit longer before he stopped answering. When she looked over, he was asleep.

Mrs. Newman met her at the door. When she peeked into the room, she chuckled. "I guess he isn't ready for more coffee?"

"No, I don't think he needs any right now." Madison laughed. "Decaf sure doesn't keep him awake. While he's sleeping, I think I'll go work on a story I need to get finished."

Madison hadn't gotten much accomplished when Adria appeared later at the door to the home office where Briggs had told her she could work.

"Hi, friend. Can I ask you a favor?" Adria smiled.

"Of course. What's up?" Madison sat back in her chair.

Adria hesitated for a moment. "Well, this is probably going to sound a little silly to you, but I'd like to see the horses. I've never... Well, I've never been close to one before, and I'd like to see them before I have to leave."

"Oh!" Madison put a hand to her mouth. "I'm sorry, Adria. I never even thought about you wanting to see the horses. I should have asked you before now."

Adria shook her head. "It's okay. You've been a little busy."

They walked over to the barn, chatting on the way there. It was empty except for the horses, since the men were all out at the big equipment barn working on the baling equipment. The two women walked down the aisle, Madison talking the whole way about the horses she had gotten to know in the last several days.

"Can I touch one of them?" Adria asked.

"Of course. We probably should go down here to MacDougal's stall. He's the friendliest. Best for a first timer." Madison gestured toward a dark chestnut gelding at the end of the row, but when she turned, a rag came over her nose and mouth from behind covering the brief hint of Adria's perfume. In little more than an instant, the world went black.

SIXTEEN

Sweat beaded Briggs's forehead by the time they finished with the baler, despite the mild midday temps. He had rolled up the sleeves of his button-down shirt long ago and now found himself wishing he had worn a T-shirt instead.

"Let's head back to the house," he told Lance. "I could use some lunch. After we eat, we'll start on the mowing machine. I'm sure it's going to need some tuning and most likely some teeth replaced on that sickle." Briggs gestured toward the attachment they would use to cut the grass before baling.

They made the trek back to the house and found Mrs. Newman had a hearty lunch of chili, beans and cornbread ready for them, but the house was otherwise nearly silent.

"Where is everyone?" Briggs washed his hands at the kitchen sink and looked around.

Mrs. Newman frowned. "Well, Jake is sleeping, but Madison and Adria went out to the barn about an hour ago to see the horses and haven't come back in yet."

Briggs nodded. "Well, they will be here anytime, then, I'm sure."

But the words settled into the pit of his stomach with an uneasy feeling. Adria had never shown any interest in the workings of the ranch before now, so he was pretty surprised she had tagged along with Madison. The two women probably shouldn't be out there alone.

He shook it off. He was probably reading too much into it. She likely just wanted to take interest in something Madison liked. Adria's ways were different to him, but it didn't mean anything was wrong with it.

They sat down to the delicious chili and

cornbread and drank an entire pitcher of sweet tea.

Mrs. Newman chuckled. "No worries, I have more."

Briggs expected the door to open and the ladies to come in at any moment, but by the time the men finished their lunch, Madison and Adria still hadn't arrived. "That's odd."

He called her cell phone. It rang several times before going to voice mail. The knot in his stomach grew. He had sent Lance into town for some parts, but he would be back in no more than fifteen minutes. He started toward the barn, but as he did so, his phone rang. Thinking it was Madison calling him back, he answered without looking at it.

"Where are you?"

Avery's voice came from the other end. "It's me, bro. Is everything okay?"

Briggs felt a deep frown tugging down the corners of his mouth. "I'm not sure yet. What's up?"

"I have a lead. I found a possible connection to the story Madison wrote exposing a drug trafficking ring a few months ago. Since the story was published, a half dozen more arrests have been made, including one John Jefferson Brady." Avery was explaining too slowly to suit Briggs.

"So what's the connection?" He was pacing now.

Avery hesitated. "The man has a daughter, and pictures I have found of the woman bear a marked resemblance to a woman who works at the newspaper."

"You think it could be her? How could she be working there and not be exposed by the story?" Briggs wasn't quite following how this could have all played out.

"The woman in question has a history of stealing people's identities, among other things. She could be posing as someone she's not. At the very least, she's a criminal working under an alias. The date of her hire lines up, also. She started working there a few months after the article was published. Her name is Adria Thomason."

It all fell into place. "I think you're right. I just hope I'm not too late." Briggs hung up and started sprinting toward the barn.

SEVENTEEN

Madison opened her eyes and had to work to force away the haze. She was bouncing roughly around in the short metal bed of the UTV Briggs kept in the barn. Everything hurt, especially her head. Her hands and feet were bound, seemingly with some sort of rope, but she couldn't move enough to see it. She struggled to remember what had happened, but only bits and pieces floated back to her. But then...

Adria.

She had stuffed a rag doused with some sort of chemical into Madison's face and mouth. But why?

She was facing the rear of the vehicle, so she couldn't see who was driving the UTV. Was it Adria? She tried to roll over so she could see, but she didn't have enough room to move, and having her hands and feet bound made it difficult to get any leverage. Eventually, she ended up scooting around on her side a little at a time while trying not to alert her captor.

Fear swam through her, clouding her thoughts and making it difficult to reason. How had she missed the signs that Adria wasn't who she said she was? Thinking back, Adria had always been close by, and she usually wasn't with her when the accidents happened. The only exception was when they had been shot at on the porch. And now that she thought back on it, Adria had seemed more angry than shaken after all that had taken place.

The most serious question plaguing her, however, was how she would escape.

Briggs was busy with the mowing and baling equipment and probably wouldn't even realize she was gone. Mrs. Newman and her father wouldn't know that Briggs wasn't with her. No one was aware of where they were. Adria hadn't given them any reason to mistrust her, surely. She had certainly had Madison fooled.

She scooted a little farther. She could almost see the front of the UTV now, and she would be able to assess what she was up against. If it were only Adria, Madison felt sure she could overtake her if she could just get her hands and feet free. If she hadn't had the element of surprise earlier, Madison could have easily fought her off, but the unexpected was hard to outsmart.

Just a little more. Her wrists and ankles ached from the pressure, and her head screamed in protest at the slightest little move. Metal dug into her back, probably fencing tools of some sort, but she couldn't squirm away from them. Still, she wriggled and jerked again, determined to increase her odds of getting away.

Her last move brought a bald head into view. Her heart sank. Madison had hoped she'd run out of hired men. She couldn't see a whole lot more than his head, though. Maybe Adria had left her in the hands of this man, whoever he was. Escaping from one man wasn't impossible, so her hopes rallied.

But before she could scoot again and verify that this was the case, she heard Adria's voice. She couldn't make out what she was saying over the drone of the UTV, but she caught a few words, none of them what she wanted to hear. Something about a tree, gun and plenty of rope. It didn't bode well, no matter how she weighed the possibilities.

Thoughts swirled around in her mind. She tried to consider the plans Adria might have for her. She seemed to be bent on revenge, though, and Madison had no idea what she could have done to her. She thought hard about all the things they had endured over the last year and a half of being friends, but Madison could think of nothing she had done to garner Adria's hatred.

One thing was certain, though. Adria was one fantastic actress, because Madison had never once suspected her.

Madison wriggled her hands, trying to work them free as quietly as she could. It was loosening a bit, but she wasn't free yet. She kept working at them while she came up with a plan. Even if she got her bindings off, she would have to escape.

Madison thought of the gate on the back of the UTV, wondering if she could trip the latch and slide out. It was risky, though, considering the speed at which the UTV was moving. And once she was free, how would she manage to flee on foot when they had the advantage of the UTV's speed? Could she get into a dense enough thicket to prevent the UTV's pursuit before they could overtake her?

She had no way of knowing how far from the ranch house they were, or even which direction Adria and her accomplice had taken her, because she didn't have a clue how long she had been unconscious. Madison wondered why Adria hadn't just killed her, since that seemed to have been the plan before. It seemed Adria was bent on letting her know what it was she had done, judging from the few words drifting back to her on the wind as the UTV sped along. A phrase that sounded like, "after what she's done to me" stuck out in Madison's mind.

She managed to stay quiet enough to not draw their attention as she scooted around just enough to see Adria beside the man in the front of the UTV.

Without warning, Adria turned, catching Madison trying to shimmy around a little to reach the latch to the tailgate with her bound hands.

"Stop the vehicle!" Adria demanded. "She's awake and trying to get away."

The short bald man laughed. "Where's she gonna go? We're miles from the house."

Well, that answered that.

"She's trying to open the tailgate. Just stop." Adria roared the words, no longer difficult to hear, thanks to her volume.

The bald man's shoulders rose and fell in what Madison could only assume was an irritated sigh, but he eased off the throttle.

"This is far enough, anyway. I think that tree over there should work just fine." Adria gestured wildly to a fat-trunked oak on her right.

"Whatever you say, sister." The man jerked the wheel, bouncing the UTV over more ruts as they made their way slowly toward the tree.

Madison struggled against her bonds, hoping to spit the foul-smelling rag from her mouth and ask what was going on, but no amount of struggle loosened either one. When the UTV stopped, Adria dropped the tailgate and demanded the man retrieve Madison from the back. When he picked her up gracelessly and tossed her over his shoulder, she couldn't hold in the grunt.

He dumped her carelessly on the ground beside the tree, and Adria demanded he hold her up where she could wrap the rope around her.

Madison wasn't about to just give in, however. She thrashed and bucked with every ounce of strength she had, fighting to resist the man's grip. He cussed and spat on the ground next to her.

"She's stronger than I thought, Gabs. Can't you make her be still? Don't you have any more of those rags to knock her out?" The bald man's voice came out as little more than a whine.

"Don't be stupid. That stuff evaporates pretty quickly after being exposed to air." Adria glared at him as if he were little more than a parasite she wanted to be done with. "Just slug her in the jaw and be done with it."

He looked at Adria for a long moment as if trying to gauge her seriousness.

"Oh for—" Adria muttered under her breath, then reared back to punch Madison.

Madison knew it was coming and managed to dodge the worst of it, despite the bald man's grip on her. That only angered Adria, and she came in for another, this time connecting soundly with Madison's chin just before everything went black once more.

* * *

Briggs couldn't believe he hadn't seen this possibility sooner.

Once he reached the barn, he didn't have to look around long before he found a suspicious white scarf wedged into a corner of the barn under a feed bag. He called the deputy to come collect the evidence. He was sure the dropped rag had something to do with Madison's disappearance. He turned in circles, his mind working.

Briggs forced himself to still a moment and think, although every instinct he had was urging him to run after Madison. But where? One deputy had been patrolling around the perimeter of the ranch, and the other had missed any suspicious activity in the barn somehow. Briggs wasn't sure what was going on there, but he suspected someone might have paid him handsomely to look the other way. The patrol deputy was on his way back to help search, but Briggs didn't know where to start.

He called Avery back. "Bro, I need some

backup. And any more info you can give me. Madison is missing."

Avery grunted. "I'm on it. Stay on the phone."

Briggs did, not surprised to find his UTV missing as he paced the barn.

"Looks like she has a half brother with quite a rap sheet." Avery spoke away from the phone on the other end, probably to their brother Beau.

"Oh, and bro, I have more bad news."

Briggs drew in a deep breath. "Let me have it."

"The woman has also a criminal record. She was eventually acquitted, but her half brother was convicted, probably because it wasn't his first arrest. Far from it. His name is Ronald James Brady, alias Ronnie Tyler. Worse, he was released from prison about a month ago. I found this when I discovered who she really is."

"What was he charged with?" Briggs was afraid to ask, but he had to.

"Kidnapping, possession of illegal drugs and paraphernalia, and attempted murder."

Avery went quiet on the other line. "We're on the way. We're not far out. Want me to call in Grayson?"

Briggs took a deep breath. His brothers, Grayson, Beau, Caldwell and Avery, could all be counted on in an emergency. All of them had worked in the military or law enforcement at some point in their lives. Briggs had hoped this could be resolved without their help, but it might be time to call in all the ammunition he could find. "Not unless we have to. He's too far away. Is Caldwell still AWOL?"

Their baby brother had disappeared from Wyoming with no word to any of them a few months ago and hadn't returned any of their calls. None of the family had spoken to him since. Briggs suspected he was still angry over a fight he had gotten into with Avery, but no one but Caldwell and Avery really knew the details.

"Yeah, I still haven't heard from him, but I'll see what I can do."

EIGHTEEN

When Madison regained consciousness again, only Adria was there with her, and she was bound to the tree, though not very neatly. She wriggled and tugged, but found no matter how poorly she was tied, the bonds were doing their job.

The UTV was gone, taking with it any hope of escape should Madison be able to somehow free herself. Adria was pacing several yards away, and though Madison wasn't sure what she had planned, a part of her wanted to call to her and get it over with. But common sense told her she should delay as long as she could to give someone time to find her.

Who was she kidding? Briggs was the only one on her mind. She had no doubt whatsoever he could save her, if only he knew where to find her. But did he even know that anything was wrong? He had no reason at all to suspect Adria. Just as Madison hadn't.

Despite the odd timing of the thought, all things considered, Briggs's kiss replayed in her mind. His tenderness, his… What? He had never said he loved her. But if she were honest, wasn't that what she was feeling for him? Already she couldn't imagine going back to her former life without him. She hadn't really taken the time to consider what she wanted for the future, but she knew it involved him and staying close to her father. If that meant giving up her life and her job in Boston, so be it. She suddenly realized the idea of that didn't bother her at all.

Madison's thoughts were interrupted when Adria turned and discovered she was alert once again. Her pacing came to an abrupt stop, and her posture took on the stalking quality of a female lioness on the hunt for her prey.

Adria sauntered over to the tree as if she had all the time she needed. Madison prayed she could keep such a calm and casual attitude. As Adria drew closer, Madison could see she held what appeared to be some type of 9 mm handgun. Adria kept it at her side, however, acting as if there was no threat to her. There probably wasn't, considering Madison didn't recognize anything around her.

"I would take off your gag so you could ask all of your questions. I know you must have plenty. But I've decided it will be easier to just tell you without interruption." Adria sighed as she stopped a few feet away. "I know how you like to ask questions."

She looked at Madison, eyes raking her up and down with disdain before turning away.

"First things first, despite how well you think you know me, my name isn't even Adria. It's Gabrielle. So you see, Madi, the person you thought you knew all along doesn't even exist." She paused. "There was an Adria Thomason once, but she disappeared. That's another story. Too bad you don't have time to do the research on her."

She smirked at Madison then.

"I do have a writing degree, however, and a very active imagination, so recreating myself as an entirely new character was actually pretty entertaining for me. I quite enjoyed it. I thought you might appreciate the effort I put into it, which is part of the reason I decided to let you in on my story before I kill you. Oh, and I guess I did base some of my character on the real Adria Thomason. She did look quite a bit like me, strangely enough."

Madison tried to swallow past the gag but almost choked instead. Had this woman already killed someone? Is that what she meant when she said the real Adria Thomason had disappeared? Chills swept through Madison.

"Now, now. None of that. I don't want you to deprive me of the pleasure of getting my revenge." Adria—or Gabrielle, or whoever this woman was—laughed low in her throat and paced before Madison, casually telling her story.

"But that wasn't the only reason. At first, I just wanted you to die. I wanted you to pay with your life for what you did. I hated you so much. But then I realized you really had no idea why I wanted you dead. Not only would you never figure out who killed you, but you wouldn't have any idea why. You didn't seem to put anything together at all. Well, now, that just wasn't acceptable to me. What would be the point, you know?"

She paused and looked at Madison. "So I decided this would be better. Besides, my half brother turned out to be the weak link in the family. He must have inherited his mother's weak genetics. Once RJ proved he and his hired friends couldn't finish the job, I came up with a new plan altogether. You'll notice I sent him away."

She gestured around her. "He had another errand, hopefully one he doesn't botch. I sent him to create a distraction just in case your little boyfriend Briggs decides to wise up. You see, he's going to turn the buffalo herd loose and scatter them all over the county to let them roam where they will. And in case that isn't enough, he's also going to poison every stupid horse in the stable."

Briggs didn't wait for Avery and Beau to get to the ranch. He called the deputies also, and they promised to provide backup. With the UTV missing from the barn, he decided to take a smaller ATV they kept in the shed. He was about to take off out the door when he noticed Thor's massive form wasn't visible in his stall.

Biting his lip on the angry words he wanted to say, he changed direction to go and look for the horse. Briggs was right next to the stall when he saw the horse lying down in the big box full of pine shavings, rolling slightly and groaning in pain.

"Ah, man. Thor, buddy, what's the matter?" He unlatched the stall door, digging his phone from his pocket as he did so. He retrieved the contact information for the vet and placed a call as he spoke softly to the horse. Dr. Tate Beckham promised to be on his way in seconds, but he had a way to drive, and Briggs didn't have seconds to wait for him to get here. He really didn't have a choice, though. He called in Lance and a couple of the other hands to be close by in case any other livestock became sick.

Was this all part of Adria's plan? It would help if he knew, because poisoning would be easier to deal with if the vet knew the cause. Briggs just prayed they weren't too late.

He called Avery back while he waited and told him what was going on.

"I'm sorry, bro." Avery sounded breathless. "We will be there in five. Sounds like you could use some extra hands. I'll tell Beau to step on it."

"Thanks, buddy. I'm glad to hear it." Briggs stroked Thor's side, trying to make him more comfortable. He had him up and was walking him around the stable, still praying the gelding would be okay so he could look for Madison.

He had little more than hung up the call with Avery when Lance called. "Boss, we have another problem. The entire bison herd is loose and wandering at will."

So much for passing the reins to Lance and going after Madison. It was all Briggs could do not to yell into the phone. "Gather them up. Take all the hands available and get them back into the pasture before anything happens to them."

It could mean the loss of the Whitsons' legacy if anything happened to that herd of bison. The loss of grants, government approval, everything could be revoked. Not to mention the hardship of losing the bison themselves. He felt anger welling up in him stronger than ever.

He hadn't felt this much rage since Wade's death.

He continued to pace with the gelding, but Thor's movements became slower and slower. Mrs. Newman appeared in the yard, Jake right behind her.

"Why didn't you tell us? We can handle the horse. Go find Madison." Mrs. Newman reached for Thor's lead rope.

Briggs didn't ask how she knew. He relinquished the lead, but Lance was coming out of the barn toward him.

"Boss, we have a couple more horses coming down sick." Lance looked ill himself having to tell Briggs.

Snowballs were one thing, but this was becoming an avalanche.

He had to think, and quickly. The bison had to be rounded up. The horses had to be treated for whatever toxin Adria had injected them with. They didn't have enough healthy horses to round up the bison, and the UTV was missing. They had only a couple of four-wheel ATVs to use. They were likely going to need more than one vet.

His military training kicked in.

"Lance, call Seth Akins and see if we can borrow any available horses and hands to get the bison rounded up. Jake, get ahold of the sheriff and tell him what's going on.

Mrs. Newman, call 911 and have Dispatch set up a barrier on the road to keep any cars from hitting stray buffalo before they can be rounded up. I'll call Dr. Beckham and tell him we might need any of his colleagues that are available today. As soon as Avery and Beau are here, I'm going to find Madison."

The entire group went into action.

By the time Beau and Avery arrived, three more horses were sick. Dr. Beckham was treating the horses as quickly as he could while waiting for his colleagues to arrive. Briggs's brothers took one look at him and told him to go.

"Get moving. We can figure out what needs to be done as we go." Avery took the lead rope Briggs was still holding and ushered his brother in the direction of the waiting ATV.

Beau also nodded, and they both turned to take on the chaos around them. More vehicles were pulling in, trailers loaded with horses, trucks with other neighbors piled inside. Briggs didn't take any more time to ponder what was actually occurring. Things were under control here.

Madison needed him.

The question was, where was she?

He knew they had to be a good distance from the ranch house, so he followed the trail out, praying for guidance along the way. Soft earth from recent rains blessed him with some tracks to help get him started, and he followed them as far as he could until the new growth of spring grasses made them difficult to discern. From there, he had to go on instinct. But prayer would help, and he intended to pray the entire way.

There was only one place on the ranch he could think of that would be remote enough to take someone to hide them out at a time like this. He knew Adria probably wouldn't know of it, but she wasn't working alone. Adria couldn't have single-handedly loaded an unconscious Madison into the UTV and hauled her away.

So he kept a lookout for the UTV and anyone else working for her along the way.

He tried to keep his mind off how long it had been since Madison had disappeared. Nothing would be gained from thinking of what could have happened to her by now. All he could do was continue to pray that God would keep her safe and give him guidance on how to save her.

Cattle raised their heads to peer at him across the greening pasture as he sped by on the ATV, going as fast as he safely could over the rutted and pockmarked landscape. He jounced and bounced as he hit gopher mounds and tufts of grass, but he didn't let up.

What was Adria's real intent? Was he too late? He didn't want to think about the fact that if Adria wanted to kill Madison, she probably could have already done so.

This was no game. Adria wanted Madison to pay with her life. He would just have to pray he could get there in time to stop her.

In the distance, he caught a glimpse of red through the trees. Just inside the shade of a tree line ahead sat the missing

UTV. The accomplice, probably Adria's half brother from what Briggs had learned, might be somewhere nearby as well.

Before he could thoroughly scan the plain to find the man, a shot echoed around him, followed a little too quickly with another. He began to move the ATV in a swerving pattern so he would be a more difficult target. He almost unconsciously took note of the direction from which the shots originated, however, and made his way close to the shooter.

He would take the guy out or die trying.

It was his hope, however, to take him alive and conscious so he could get some answers from the man. Hopefully, he would get more from him than the police had gotten from the hired men they'd captured so far. Briggs was confident the man would know where Madison was, and any navy SEAL was well-versed in methods of making people talk.

He just hoped he didn't have to use them.

When he got close enough, he swerved into the cover of the trees, which thankfully weren't too terribly thick with undergrowth yet this early in the year. It was tight in places, but he managed to get into cover. He pulled his gun out as he bailed off and dropped low, leaving the engine running. The deputy who had promised backup should be close behind him.

Briggs saw the man move in the distance, hoping his adversary hadn't spotted him yet. He kept the guy in his sights.

Easing his way along, Briggs tried to keep quiet. Another random shot was fired as he inched along on the ground, staying as low as he possibly could. He didn't think the man could see him, so Briggs suspected the shooter was just trying to scare him away. Still, getting this close was a huge risk.

Briggs swung out, approaching wide and making his way around behind the man, his Glock at the ready. The man wasn't even aware of what Briggs had done. He was still looking for Briggs's approach from the ATV when Briggs leaped at him from behind, catching him in a relentless choke hold.

The element of surprise had the bald man dropping his weapon and grasping for the strong forearm locked around his neck. He grunted and struggled against Briggs for a little bit and then began to go helplessly limp. Just before he passed out, Briggs loosened his hold just enough to keep the man breathing and conscious.

"Tell me where she is." Briggs growled low in his ear. "Tell me where to find Madison and I will let you breathe."

The man coughed weakly and sputtered. He didn't answer, though.

Briggs tightened his grip again. "Where is she?"

Whether it was the increased intensity of his voice, or the threat of losing oxygen again, the man began to writhe. "Okay!"

Briggs barely understood the word, but the body language was easy to interpret. He would cooperate. Somewhat.

"I know they aren't far away, or you

wouldn't be standing guard." Briggs jerked his forearm into the man's jugular once more.

"No. Not far." The words tumbled out desperately.

"Where?"

"I'll take you to them. Just let me go." The bald man's voice wheezed.

"Nice try. You're not going anywhere." With his other hand, Briggs twisted the man's arm around hard behind his back. The man yelped and then screamed like an injured animal. "Except maybe back to prison. Ronnie, is it?"

The man's posture slumped, all the fight going out of him. "Just on the other side of this tree line, there is a small ridge. Under that is a big oak tree. That's where I left them. But you're probably too late."

Briggs slackened his hold. "I need some insurance to make sure you aren't lying. You're going with me. If it's some sort of trap, you'll be the first to suffer."

Briggs forced Ronnie to walk over to the

UTV and then pulled both his hands behind his back. He trussed the man up with some heavy-duty baling twine and used a pull-chain for the tractors to lock him onto the UTV. He double-checked him for additional weapons and then started the UTV.

As he punched the throttle and drove out of the trees in the direction the man had told him he would find Madison, he uttered a prayer that he wasn't too late.

He didn't know when it had happened or how, but something had changed between him and Madison. Something had changed with *him*. He had to find Madison in time and tell her how he felt, that he was desperately in love with her.

Because he couldn't even consider life without Madison in it.

NINETEEN

Madison shrank back as Adria—or Gabrielle—yelled in her face.

"Your stupid story ruined my life! Because of you, I had to go into hiding. After they arrested my father, I lost everything, and they came for me. The men—ruthless men who my father had always protected me from—came after me. Do you know how terrifying that was?"

She paused in her pacing to glare at Madison.

Of course, Madison couldn't answer because she was still bound and gagged. She had no idea who this woman's father was, or what ruthless men she was ranting about. Her confusion must have shown on her face.

"Let me go further back, Madison. You wrote a story, an exclusive that scooped every other reporter in the nation, that exposed a drug trafficking ring as it was busted. The ringleader had already been arrested, but once your story was published, the information you had gathered led to many other arrests. One of those men was my father, John Jefferson Brady. He had worked so hard to cover his tracks, too. Once the ringleader was taken to prison and things began to die down, he thought everything was going to be fine. He was in hiding, had changed his identity, gone through all the necessary precautions…but because of your story, it wasn't enough."

She looked like she wanted to spit on Madison at this last revelation. It seemed this woman before her had turned into a totally different person, someone Madison had never known.

"They took him to prison. The government seized my home, the money and all our other worldly possessions. I had nothing left. And even worse, my father will be in prison for the rest of his life. How would you like to live without your father, Madison?" She gave an evil laugh. "You almost got to find out. I wish I had switched out those pills sooner. It would have been nice to see you suffer."

Madison just stared at her, unable to speak, but she knew pity had to be shining from her eyes along with the horror of knowing what lengths the woman had gone to in order to hurt Madison. This poor lost woman actually thought that her father's arrest was Madison's fault, rather than the result of the decisions he had made. What could lead someone to such corrupt thinking?

"Don't look at me like that, Madison. I know now more than ever that you don't have any idea what it's like to have anything other than a perfect life. You were raised here, in a place like this, with good people you could count on. You don't know what it's like to have to try to survive. Sure, you lost your mother and your friend Wade, but you've never had to suffer. You've never had anything but peace and beauty in your charmed, fairy-tale life. You got the job you wanted, the notoriety, and you were about to get the charming prince as well. Too bad he's too late."

To emphasize her point, the woman pulled out the gun she had gripped earlier, hands shaking as she did so. She used her left hand to pull the gag from Madison's mouth. "Any last words, Madi dear?"

She sneered, but it didn't deter Madison.

"Yes. You don't have to do this. We can get you help. We can make your life better. Don't throw away the friendship that we had over this. Those choices that your father made were his, not yours. And he did *choose* that path. He sent himself to prison by making those choices." Madison tried to keep the quaver from her voice, but she knew this was her last shot. Her words were true, and she could only pray the woman would accept them.

She screamed instead. "*No!* You don't get it. You don't get any of it."

She raised the gun and put it against Madison's forehead, pressing the cold nose of the barrel into her skin. "We were never friends. It was a lie. I've always hated you. So. Much."

Madison took a chance. She knew it was risky. "Maybe you didn't intend for it to happen, but I was your friend. I loved you, Adria. And you were a friend to me, whether you meant to be one or not."

She shook her head violently then. "No. No one loves me. Adria isn't even really my name. You loved someone who didn't exist."

"That's not true." Madison kept her voice soft and even. "Adria does exist. I know not all of it was a lie. There is a good person in there somewhere."

The woman squeezed her eyes shut, still shaking her head in denial, but she slowly lowered the gun, hands trembling at an alarming rate as she did so. "There isn't, though. Not anymore. There is too much disappointment. Too much cynicism and hatred."

She took a few steps away, still holding the gun precariously at her side.

"It doesn't have to be that way." Madison kept her voice low, still afraid of spooking her again. "Make the decision to change. You know Briggs is probably going to be here any moment. We can get you a deal with the prosecutor and get you some help."

Anger and rage filled the woman's face again unexpectedly. "That's enough from you." She shoved the gag back into Madison's mouth. "Unfortunately, this is going to be a messy business. I don't have great aim, but I understand shooting at close range can make up for that."

She started walking back toward Madison but stopped short when the sound of an ATV interrupted her trek.

"I told RJ to stay put until I came to get him. What's that idiot doing?"

But the ATV never appeared. In fact, the sound faded into the distance. Madison's hopes rose and fell once again as she realized Briggs could be looking for her, but if he was, he had passed right by her.

"Ugh. That idiot. He's supposed to be keeping watch." Adria gripped the gun and took off sprinting over the ridge.

Madison used the opportunity to struggle fiercely against her bonds, trying to loosen them enough to shimmy free. They held surprisingly well, but she kept trying. She had to get loose. There was no reasoning with this woman right now, and she prayed she could get free before it was too late. Madison closed her eyes and leaned outward with all her might, trying desperately to generate enough force to at least loosen the ropes. With a final grunt, she went slack in disgust.

Tears threatened, but Madison fought them back. She wouldn't let her win. Madison wasn't going to give Adria, Gabrielle, whoever she was, such satisfaction. There had to be a way out of this, and she wouldn't give up until she found it.

She thought hard, knowing her time was short. No doubt her captor would soon be back with reinforcements. She kept trying to shimmy her shoulders and loosen the ropes. Her hands were tied separately, so she knew if she could get even one loose, she would have something to work with. The rope was wrapped around and around her body several times, though, and she wasn't sure how she would ever get one arm free enough to use it.

After a few minutes of struggle, however, she gained a little bit of hope. She was sure the rope was slightly looser than before, and she fought against it with a renewed vigor. She grunted and gasped as she tried to work the limb free. She was so intent on her goal that she didn't even realize she wasn't alone until she heard her name spoken barely above a whisper.

Her head shot up, and she looked straight into Briggs's eyes as he rushed toward her.

"Come on. We don't have much time. I led her on a bit of a wild goose chase, but she'll catch up to us if we don't hurry. The ATV is hidden, but her brother is tied to it, and we have to get to him before she does or she'll free him," Briggs explained as he cut her free.

"You should have taken him to the authorities," Madison said. She felt the blood rushing back into her freed limbs. She realized her words made no sense, but she had too much going on in her head right now. The sight of Briggs was like a dream, and her senses hadn't figured out how to respond just yet.

So she kissed him.

He chuckled as he pulled away. "I'm happy to see you, too. But we have to hurry. Later."

They raced across the field, his raw strength and endurance amazing her. She tried to keep up, but he pulled her along. They reached the ATV just before the gunshots began. They dropped low and dove into the vehicle, trying to get moving before Madison's captor could improve her aim.

Madison squeezed in between the driver's seat and Briggs's captive, who glared at her viciously. She scooted down behind him, using him as a shield. When she did, the shots soon stopped and changed direction, seemingly aimed at the tires now.

Before long, they were out of range and back at the ranch, and when the deputy finally arrived, he arrested Gabrielle's brother. Madison was afraid to breathe a sigh of relief, though. She knew it wasn't over.

Briggs called the second deputy, who was still on patrol. He updated the officer and got him on the search for Gabrielle around the perimeter, just in case she decided to try to flee. And then Briggs said the words Madison didn't want to hear.

"Stay here with my brothers. I'm going after her."

Briggs had no time to waste. There was no doubt in his mind that anyone who would plan something so elaborate and go so far to deceive and get close to someone wouldn't give up easily. He had to find Gabrielle. Desperation made people do terrible things. He knew from experience, unfortunately.

Madison was having none of it. She didn't want him to go alone.

"Briggs, you need someone there to help you. What if you're injured? What if you just need an extra set of hands? It's not smart to go alone. Let me come." She pleaded with her eyes as well as her voice.

She had a point. Even in the SEALs, they learned to always have someone on their six, watching their back. The unexpected happened far too often, and though he thought Gabrielle's half brother was her only accomplice on the scene, there was still a chance she had other help.

Everyone else was still very busy trying to coral the chaos. He didn't have time to waste.

Still, it might be too risky. "I don't know if that's a good idea. Maybe it would be better if you stayed here."

Madison's face was full of fear. "What if there is someone else involved? Am I safe here without you? Everyone's pretty busy."

He looked around. She was right. He was going to need to take a deputy to bring Gabrielle back into custody, anyway, leaving one less man to protect her.

He gave in with a sigh. "Fine. But we need to take Jamie with us." He was referring to the younger deputy who had taken over for Carl. He was the one patrolling the perimeter of the ranch.

Once they located Jamie, they buckled back into the ATV and sped over the landscape once again, this time taking a shortcut to the area where they had last seen Gabrielle. Jamie followed at a short distance. There was a good chance she had found the UTV she and her brother had taken Madison in by now, so he tried to listen for it over the whine of their ATV's engine.

He saw a flash of red bounce across the grass toward them it before he heard the UTV. Gabrielle must have seen them, too, however, because she turned and sped straight for them.

Briggs swerved when he realized she

intended to ram into them. She swerved more toward him as well, narrowly missing them. Madison held on tightly to the seat, letting out a tiny shriek when they nearly collided.

Gabrielle wasn't finished, though. She turned the UTV and came back for them. She was quicker on the larger machine and managed to ram them in the back fender this time before Briggs could get completely out of her path.

The ATV bounced and spun out, but Briggs managed to keep it upright. Madison let out a sharp gasp beside him and held on more tightly. Before they could fully recover, Gabrielle was on them again, this time catching them at just the right angle to overturn their machine.

Landing roughly on the side, the vehicle rocked a couple of times, then settled, thankfully without much drama. Briggs looked Madison over carefully as he unfastened his seat belt to go after Gabrielle. Jamie, who had been following in the sheriff patrol SUV, jumped out to help Briggs and Madison.

"Are you okay?" Briggs pulled out his gun as he scrambled over the side of the overturned ATV.

"I'm fine, just getting a little angry about all her shenanigans." Madison huffed out the words.

Briggs spared her an amused look. "Only just now?"

"Well, not really." Madison scrambled out after him.

Jamie coughed as he and Briggs took off after Gabrielle on foot.

Gabrielle was speeding toward Madison again, but Briggs took aim and blew out a front tire. The UTV rolled clumsily, spitting Gabrielle out of the side opening of the machine before almost landing on top of her. Madison had jumped behind the SUV to get out of Gabrielle's path, and she peeked out just in time to see the wreck.

Gabrielle screamed, and Briggs dove toward her. The UTV's engine whined in the background as he wrestled the weapon she had somehow managed to keep hold of. Jamie had his Ruger out and ran in to help out.

She just kept screaming in rage and fighting him like a wildcat until Briggs finally got her secured. Jamie was there to cuff her and drag her to the SUV.

"Look who's here." Briggs nodded toward an unfamiliar truck bouncing over the pasture toward them.

Madison smiled. "Your hands coming to save the day?"

Briggs shook his head as he realized who was behind the wheel. "My brothers. Well, two of the four, anyway."

As Avery and Beau got out of the truck, Briggs went to meet them. He was glad to see them, not just for their help, but because he had missed them over the last several weeks.

"This is Avery, the baby," Briggs said, and his younger brother puffed out his chest in mild protest.

"He means I'm the youngest." Avery put out a hand, though.

"But you're also the baby," Beau chimed in. "I'm Briggs's twin, by the way."

He grinned at Madison, and Briggs glared back at him. "Watch it, brother."

"Let's get your captive back to civilization. Looks like she put up a bit of a fight." Avery nodded at the wreckage.

As Jamie stuffed her into the SUV, Gabrielle was still spitting venomous remarks that they all ignored, and Briggs grunted. "She's still trying to."

Madison looked away, and Briggs felt a stab of regret for her. He looked over to their captive. This didn't even look like the woman who had come to the ranch under the guise of friendship. Gabrielle's once neatly groomed, long dark hair was a mass of tangles. Her makeup was smeared and streaked all over her face. Her outside finally reflected the mess that seemed to be going on inside of her.

Briggs was filling with sympathy for Madison, as well as worry. This kind of betrayal might make it difficult for her to accept what he wanted to say to her, but he couldn't deny it any longer.

She was probably going to need some time to understand how much she meant to him. How was he ever going to get her to stay?

TWENTY

Madison stood with Briggs and his brothers as the officers loaded Gabrielle into the police car. She wasn't sure when she had started thinking of the woman by her real name, but it helped a little not to think of her as the friend she once thought Adria to be.

It hurt. It hurt in ways Madison couldn't have understood if she hadn't experienced it. But she would move on.

She uttered a quick prayer, both for Gabrielle and for herself, that it could somehow be a new beginning for them both. Yes, Gabrielle's actions were going to have serious repercussions, but Madison prayed she could be healed one day of whatever had scarred her so tragically.

Madison was going to need healing from this new wound as well. It was the worst kind of betrayal, and she felt ridiculously inadequate after believing in someone so deceptive.

Briggs walked slowly toward her as his brothers loaded in the truck to head back to the ranch house, taking his hat off as he approached. He looked down until he got close, and when their eyes met, she realized this was what true goodness looked like. Peace whispered over her like a caress. There could be no doubt about the goodness of this man.

Madison smiled at him. "Thank you."

"Thank you?" He looked mildly insulted.

"Yes, thank you." She laughed then. "For everything."

Briggs frowned at her, his steely jaw set for a moment. "That's not really the kind of thanks I had hoped for."

"Hmm." Madison looked up at him. "Well, I'm not sure what sort of thanks you were expecting."

He searched her face and then wrapped

his arms around her. His embrace felt warm, secure and very much like home. "This is a good place to start."

She tilted her head sideways for a moment before leaning close to touch her lips to his. "Thank you."

"Getting warmer," Briggs teased.

She laughed, drawing closer once more, and he captured her lips more fully and kissed her thoroughly. She melted against him and let his kiss deepen.

"Now that's a proper thank-you." Briggs eased back and grinned down at her.

"I'm not sure I should go around thanking people like that." Madison put a finger to her cheek, pretending to ponder the question.

"No, definitely not." Briggs pulled away, feigning surprise. "This was a special case."

"How do I know when it's a special case, then?" Madison drew him close again.

"It's pretty simple, really. Only when it's me you're thanking." Briggs kissed her again. "And better yet, only me forever."

Madison felt her eyes widen as she pulled back a little ways to look into his face. "Briggs?"

"I guess I need to start over." He grasped her hands. "I know it's probably the worst possible time with all that has just happened, but I can't wait any longer to tell you. I love you, Madison. I want you to stay."

Her heart seemed to swell into her throat. "Briggs, there's a lot to think about."

"I know. But…when I thought I might lose you, I realized I couldn't bear it. I know I haven't exactly been giving with my heart. I haven't really been the romantic or emotional type. But I have realized you have already become the most important thing in my life." His blue eyes gazed into hers with a fierce intensity.

Her heart stuttered. "I love you, too, Briggs. All I could think of out there was you."

He kissed her gently. "Stay. I know your father would love it, too."

Madison smiled. "I'd love to. But I need to go back for now. What about my job?"

"There are reporter jobs here. You can write anywhere, right? Or you can help me run the ranch. You're okay on a horse." Briggs grasped her hand, grinning at her.

"Are you asking me what I think you're asking me?" Madison was afraid to hope. Could he truly want her to stay forever?

"Yes. I am." Briggs slid to one knee, drawing her hand with him. "Madison Burke, will you marry me? I promise to be your protector and sidekick from now until forever. If you'll have me."

"Yes!" Madison gasped. "Yes, I will marry you, Briggs!"

He pulled her to him and kissed her. "I kinda need to get you a ring."

They both laughed.

"A ring from you sounds perfect, Briggs Thorpe."

She let him pull her toward him again, kissing her sweetly and wrapping his arms around her tightly. His embrace felt like everything she had ever wanted. It was home. *She* was home.

When they finally made it back to the house, Briggs's jaw dropped at the swarm of people buzzing around the ranch. It seemed the whole community was there helping with the bison and the horses. Neighbors he had only met a time or two worked opposite friends and family. The bison seemed to all be safely back in the pasture, the fences were repaired where needed, and his veterinarian approached him about the horses.

"Looks like all of the horses are going to recover just fine. It might take the older ones a little longer to regain their strength, but they should all be back to normal very soon. Since the poisoning was discovered quickly, it shouldn't have any lasting effects." Dr. Beckham shook the hand Briggs offered.

"Thank you, Dr. Beckham. I appreciate it. And thank you for getting here so quickly." Briggs dropped his hand. "I'm sure it made all the difference."

"No problem, Briggs. If any complications arise, give me a call." He nodded and went back to the barn.

Madison appeared beside him, looking tired and happy. "It looks like this community has accepted you as one of their own. They really showed up for you."

"I'm awestruck, to be honest." Briggs was still looking around at them all.

"They've always been that way around here. It seems some things never change." Madison's gaze scanned the buzz of activity as well.

"In this case, that's definitely a good thing." Briggs turned to her then. "There is one person I need to find, though. Have you seen your father?"

"He's in the barn with Thor." Madison blushed, probably knowing full well what he wanted to talk to her father about.

"Great. And, Madison?" He added the last with a serious expression.

"Yes?" Madison returned his seriousness.

"Don't let either of my brothers try to steal you away before I get back." He winked at her and nodded at the approaching pair.

He noticed her flush deepened even more just before he walked away.

He found Jake speaking softly to his big gelding, just as Madison had said he did. He approached slowly and cleared his throat. "I'd like to talk to you if you have a minute."

Jake took one look at him and grinned. "Oh, finally! What took you so long?"

Briggs felt his face heat. "How did—"

Jake was already shaking his head. "I'm not obtuse, just good at pretending."

Briggs cleared his throat again. "Well. I guess…"

"Ask already, would ya?" Jake teased him.

He grinned, feeling off his game. "I'd like to marry your daughter, sir."

He expected a handshake. Maybe a clap on the shoulder. But he didn't expect the bear hug Jake wrapped him in. "I would be lying if I said I hadn't hoped for this very thing long before you two even met. Of course you have my permission to marry her. And congratulations, son."

"Thank you, sir. I'll do my best to take care of her."

Briggs wasted no time finding Madison again and taking her into his arms. "I just had the best conversation with your dad."

"Oh? Please tell me what it was about." Madison smiled as he leaned in for a kiss.

Before his lips touched hers, however, he felt the smile he couldn't hold back stretching over his face. "We have his blessing. And I can't wait to marry you."

"Well, I can't see any reason to wait, either. Let's plan the wedding right away."

He answered by kissing her soundly.

EPILOGUE

Madison was happier than she had ever been.

She and Briggs were married on the ranch, with all their friends, family, and new acquaintances they had met in their time of crisis in attendance. It was late summer, and the wind across the open fields had begun to have a slight coolness to it, something slightly crisp in anticipation of the coming fall.

Madison knew she was being fanciful, but she was so sure she could feel her mother's presence here with her today. She was here in the wind, in the sun, and wrapping all around her. She smiled to herself.

All of Briggs's brothers were in attendance, as well as his new sister-in-law,

Lauren, and his adopted niece, Riley. Madison had been fascinated to learn that Lauren and Grayson had protected Riley after she had nearly been abducted from the hospital as a newborn. She and Lauren learned they had much in common when it came to being protected by Thorpe brothers.

Her father gave Madison away, whispering that her mother would be so proud of her, and he stood smiling with Mrs. Newman while the ceremony took place. At one point, she thought she saw him squeeze the older woman's hand, and Madison was hopeful that something was blooming between them. It was time for her father to move on with his life. She couldn't think of anyone she would rather have her father marry than Mrs. Newman.

Her father had received good news from the doctor on his last visit, and a minor surgery was scheduled for him that should give him a much better chance at getting back to normal. His medication had been working well, and the doctor had given him a good prognosis. Nevertheless, he was retiring as ranch foreman, and though Briggs had tried to get him to live at the ranch, he'd purchased a small house close by, wanting to give the couple some privacy.

Madison had resigned from the newspaper and accepted a job writing for a Western journal, chronicling the restoration of the buffalo herds, among other things. She was more than happy to give up city life to help Briggs out on the ranch.

Wade's mother was also able to attend the ceremony under the watchful care of a nurse, and she and Madison shared a few laughs and tears over her son's memory. Mrs. Whitson had made Madison feel a little less lonely for her mother as well.

Mrs. Whitson was about to leave but took a moment to say goodbye to the couple at the reception. "Madison, you've always been a part of this ranch. I'm so happy to see you back here. It's where you belong." She squeezed her hand and turned to Briggs. "You've done well with everything. Thank you for preserving my husband's legacy."

Briggs turned a little pink, and Madison almost teared up at her words, but then his brothers approached and began to rib him about being an old married man now. Riley reached for him, and Lauren pulled Madison into a hug.

"Finally, I'm not so outnumbered by all these men!" Lauren smiled at her.

"You're still outnumbered, just not as much." Avery winked at his two sisters-in-law. "We just need to keep it that way."

"Well, as long as you guys are all wrapped around the finger of that little lady right there, I think she will have all the power." Lauren nodded toward Riley, who had three of her uncles acting plumb silly over her.

Madison laughed. "For sure."

Avery threw up his hands. "I can't argue with that."

"You'd better watch yourself, Avery. Any of you boys could be next." Lauren laughed, giving her brother-in-law a little hug.

"Not me. I'm good." Avery shook his head as if appalled at the thought.

Briggs came up beside Madison then. "That's what we all said, brother. But just wait. I realized I didn't even know what good was."

He leaned down and gave Madison a light kiss and whispered to her alone, "I love you, Madison Thorpe. I can't wait to spend forever with you."

Her eyes filled, and her chest expanded as she returned his kiss. "I love you, too."

Contentment swelled within her, and she wrapped her arms around her husband more tightly. *Her husband.*

She had never heard anything sweeter than those words.

* * * * *

If you enjoyed Ranch Under Siege,
*pick up these other thrilling stories
by Sommer Smith:*

Under Suspicion
Attempted Abduction

*Available now from
Love Inspired Suspense!
Find more great reads at
www.LoveInspired.com.*

Dear Reader,

Thank you for joining me on another Thorpe Brothers adventure. Protecting Madison gave Briggs a new sense of purpose after leaving the SEALs. Raising buffalo, too, made him feel needed. Thanks to the efforts of the Wildlife Conservation Society, the population of the American bison is now stable, though they were endangered for some time. These historic animals still face threats related to loss of habitat and low genetic diversity, however. It is sad to think these majestic creatures have lost so much of their home. There are modern-day ranchers who are helping to preserve the American bison, though, and I am thankful for their efforts.

Do let me know what you thought of the inclusion of buffalo, as well as the rest of the story, by contacting me at ssmith. kgc3@gmail.com.

I hope you loved the story!

Blessings!
Sommer Smith